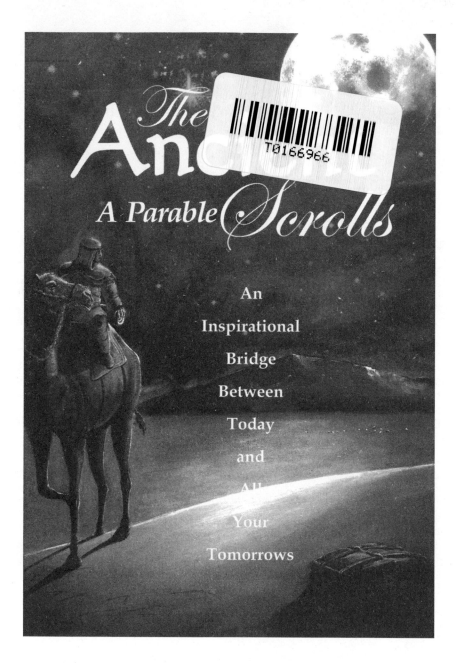

The Ancient Scrolls

A Parable

An
Inspirational
Bridge
Between
Today
and
All
Your
Tomorrows

Tim Connor, CSP

FREDERICK FELL PUBLISHERS, INC.

2131 Hollywood Boulevard - Suite # 305

Hollywood, Florida 33020

954-925-5242

e-mail: fellpub@aol.com

Visit our web site at www.fellpub.com

This publication is designed to provide accurate and authoritative information in regard to the subject matter covered. It is sold with the understanding that the publisher is not engaged in rendering legal, accounting, or other professional service. If legal advice or other assistance is required, the services of a competent professional person should be sought. From A Declaration of Principles jointly adopted by a Committee of the American Bar Association and a Committee of Publishers.

Library of Congress Cataloging-in-Publication Data

Connor, Tim 1942-
 The Ancient Scrolls, A Parable: An Inspirational Bridge Between Today and All Your Tomorrows/ By Tim Connor.
p. cm.
ISBN: 0-88391-073-X (pbk.)
1. Conduct of Life. I. Title.
BJ1597 C66 2002
170`.44--dc21

                              2002010896

10 9 8 7 6 5 4 3 2 1

Interior and Cover Design by Chris Hetzer

The Ancient Scrolls

A Parable

Books by Tim Connor

Soft Sell

The Voyage

Crossroads

The Mission

That's Life

Sales Mastery

The Trade-Off

Win-Win Selling

52 Tips For Success

The Ancient Scrolls

The Road to Happiness

The Road to Happiness – Fun Book

Assignment Workbooks

How to Sell MORE in LESS Time

Your First year in Sales

Daily Success Journal

Walk Easy With me Through Life

Lead, Manage or Get Out of The Way

Let's Get Back To Basics Series

*Let the great world spin
for ever down the ringing grooves of
change.*
     Lord Tennyson

The Ancient Scrolls

-A parable-

An inspirational bridge between today and all your tomorrow's.

Tim Connor

The Ancient Scrolls

Life is like the seasons...

There is winter...
> *filled with regrets and pain.*

There is springtime...
> *filled with hope and sewing.*

There is summer...
> *Filled with fun and opportunity.*

And There is Fall...
> *Filled with Joy and reaping.*

The seasons come and go. Life ebbs and flows.
We cannot change the seasons.

> *We enjoy their passing.*

We cannot see the future.

we can only enjoy the present,
> *one moment at a time.*

Tim Connor,CSP

In memory

Of Og Mandino, my friend, mentor,
and Hero who gave me the inspiration
and courage to stretch my
writing into uncharted seas.
I miss you Og, we all miss you.

Forward

For centuries, the first 12 ancient scrolls were the foundation for success in business and in life.

Suddenly there is a new discovery by a well-known caravan owner that will change the course of history.

The Ancient Scrolls is a story that will entertain you as it helps you look inside for the answers to many of today's life challenges.

In *The Ancient Scrolls,* you will discover your purpose and destiny in life. It will give you a renewed sense of motivation and enthusiasm as it guides you through a thought provoking process that will end with increased happiness and resolve.

The Ancient Scrolls is a timeless story that has a significant message today for everyone in society who has a need and desire to better influence others.

If you are searching for a better tomorrow, more fulfilling relationships, career or business success, and a clearer understanding of the meaning of your life, *The Ancient Scrolls* was written for you....

You are now holding in your hand a book that can change the course of the rest of your life!!

Everyone everywhere, regardless of their position, experience, age, sex, economic status and past history, needs to better influence and persuade others.

Whether you - are managing people, raising children, selling products, services or ideas, looking for a better career position, own a business, teach, or any number of professions or activities - the ability to effectively get your ideas across is a critical skill.

I will wager that if you were successful at anything today that involved other people, you effectively influenced or persuaded them. If you were not, you need to improve this ability.

The Ancient Scrolls is a tool that can help you get what you want from life. It is the story of the search for better understanding, personal power and success - however you choose to define it. It is a book that will become a treasured friend for years to come.

Introduction

This is a story that can change your life. It is a parable.

It is about the transformation of your life and career from an intellectual, focused approach to a heart centered approach.

Woven throughout these pages are countless pearls of wisdom from the ages that can have a dramatic impact on your life.

Everyone sells everyday. Teachers, parents, spouses, politicians, clerics, professionals, and children all sell. Selling is not just about moving products, services or ideas. Rather, it's the ability to influence and persuade others.

Whether you are selling a prospective employer on your skills, or your sweetheart on a committed relationship, the rules are the same.

Some people have mastered these skills, and live a life filled with peace, happiness, freedom, and prosperity. Others have not studied or practiced them, and lead lives of frustration, anxiety, and disappointment.

Let your imagination run free. Resist the tendency to judge, criticize or compare. This philosophy is ego-centered. Enjoy the process of your awareness unfolding as it takes place throughout these pages.

The story is both timeless and timely. Its truths are just as relevant today as they were several thousand years ago when this story took place!

Chapter One

Many years ago in a far off land, there was a king without a castle.

This king was called by the name of Harold.

He grew up under the influence of his father. All Harold ever wanted was a kingdom and castle of his own. When he turned twenty-one he began his search for the finest castle available in the land.

He thought long and hard about what he wanted his castle to look like, how much he could afford, and where he wanted it to be. He knew that somewhere out in the kingdom there was a castle that would meet all his desires and needs as he established his own kingdom far from his father's castle.

Harold spent many months researching castle architecture, location, resale values, and the demographics of several potential areas where he might one day settle down, find his princess, and live happily ever after.

He researched, and then contacted several well known castle merchants who he believed could assist him with his search, and he set up appointments with each of them.

Several years after purchasing his castle, King Harold was walking in one of his gardens with his chief of castle operations. He shared the trials and tribulations of his earlier search with his trusted friend, Mahmoud.

"Mahmoud, the following scenarios are true in every detail. When I am finished I would like your comments on my experience."

"Harold, it will be my pleasure to offer you my feedback. Please begin."

"As you know Mahmoud, it took me several years to finally locate and purchase our current castle. I was to discover much later that it wasn't necessary to have taken that long, but I was forced to deal with a rather unprofessional group of castle merchants. Let me share with you my experiences with just three of them.

"Merchant number one came from the east. He traveled many miles to sell me a castle. Prior to his journey, he sent me a great deal of literature about his organization and many castles that he knew would interest me. His journey from the east lasted many days. When he arrived he was weary, hungry, and in need of making the sale. He seemed troubled and desperate. I never read the material he sent me. By the time it arrived by camel, it was dirty, outdated, and in no way represented what I believed was in my best interests. Since he had traveled so far, I decided to grant him an audience.

"He spent many hours telling me of his virtues and the virtues of his organization. We looked at many of the castles he represented, but none were quite what I was looking for. He tried to close the sale with one of the ancient closes.

"He asked me, 'do you want the castle in the forest or the one on the hill?

"I told him neither, and advised him to return to his home in the east, and that he search for the truths in the ancient Scrolls. He departed broken and discouraged, never knowing what he had done wrong."

"Harold, why did you not buy from this merchant?"

"Mahmoud, my old friend, he broke every rule that has been passed on for generations in the ancient Scrolls."

"What are those rules?"

"I will share them with you at the end of our discussion."

"And what of the second merchant?"

"He came from the west. He also traveled far, but he at least arrived refreshed and in good spirits. When he entered my chamber, he had the biggest smile I have ever seen. He was One of the friendliest merchants I have ever met. We talked about much trivia. I found out more about him than I would have ever wanted to know.

"He invited me to lunch at a local café in the village. He should have known that kings never eat with the peasants. It is an age-old tradition. Kings only venture out on special holidays and celebrations. But I broke one of my rules, and left the castle with him. He was a very nice person. He talked a great deal throughout lunch.

"He seemed to be in need of much recognition and approval. After we finished lunch, he asked me if I would like to join him at the local jousting match. Now Mahmoud, you know that I hate jousting."

"Did you join him at the match?"

"I did."

"Why?"

"I felt obligated. He traveled far, and purchased lunch. I did not want to hurt his feelings."

"Harold, when did you look at castles?"

"You know Mahmoud, that is the strangest thing. We never did. He said he would visit me again in several weeks and we would then look at nearby castles."

"Did he ever return?"

"No. I told him that I had already visited each of the castles within one hundred miles, to save his time."

"What happened next?"

"Well I did receive a very nice letter from him thanking me for my time and hospitality. He said the next time I was in need of castle to give him a call."

"Harold, did he also break several of the rules in the ancient Scrolls?"

"Yes, he broke many."

"what of the third merchant?"

"He came from the north. But before making his trip, he sent me a letter asking me of my needs, interests, likes, dislikes, and many other particulars that I wanted in my new castle. When he arrived we spent many hours talking about my research, experiences, and investigation, as well as his interest in helping me. Mahmoud, I must tell you that I knew very little personally about this merchant, but I know one thing!"

"And what is that?"

"I trusted him. He was more interested in me, my needs, and my desires than just selling me a castle. I liked him also, but I bought my castle from him not because I liked him, but because he cared more about me than himself, available castles, or his organization."

"Did you negotiate the price of the castle?"

"That is another strange thing. I felt as though it was not necessary to do so. I believed him when he told me that the price of the castle was a fair one and that the price, although important, was secondary to my comfort, happiness and safety. I never doubted his counsel for a minute. He told me that he would stop by from time to time when he was in my kingdom to ensure my continued satisfaction."

"has he honored his commitment to do so?"

"Yes, as a matter of fact, he will be joining us for lunch today. I have asked him to find me a cottage in the forest for those times when we have foreign dignitaries that will be staying with us, and would like to get away from the noise and chaos of the city. He says he has a perfect one for us to visit today."

"How does he know it is perfect without your seeing it first?"

"He knows because he has followed all the rules in the ancient scrolls."

"Harold, when will I get to see the scrolls?"

"I have asked him to bring a copy for you. I know you will want to study them before you embark on your journey."

"I didn't know I was going on a journey."

"I want you to visit every corner of our kingdom in search of the best merchants. Those that have studied the scrolls and put them to use. When you have finished your mission, I want you to return with whomever meets our criteria. I have an exciting adventure in store for you, and your newly discovered group."

The merchant arrived and asked if they were ready to visit the small castle he had chosen for harold.

After purchasing the cottage, they returned to the castle. the salesperson left the king and shared the scrolls with Mahmoud in his quarters. after which, Mahmoud departed on his journey to the far corners of the kingdom in search of merchants who lived by the truth found in the ancient Scrolls.

The Ancient Scrolls

Scroll Number One:
People buy from people they trust.

Scroll Number Two:
People buy from people who care.

Scroll Number Three:
People buy from people who ask.

Scroll Number Four:
People buy from people who listen.

Scroll Number Five
People buy from people who plan.

Scroll Number Six:
People buy from people who pay attention.

Scroll Number Seven:
People buy from people who honor their promises.

Scroll Number Eight:
People buy from people who sell value not price.

Scroll Number Nine:
People buy from people who are a resource for them.

Scroll Number Ten:
People buy from people who promise a lot and deliver more.

Scroll Number Eleven:
People buy from people who invest in themselves.

Scroll Number Twelve:
People buy from people who work as hard to keep the business
as they did to get it.

Chapter Two

Mahmoud had been gone for many months. There was no word from him, and the king began to worry that Mahmoud had failed in his mission. But there was nothing he could do but wait. And waiting was not something he liked to do.

In the early days of his journey, Mahmoud met with much disappointment and rejection. He visited dozens of shops and merchants in the cities, and he even traveled with several caravans. All with no success. He was beginning to think that there were no merchants anywhere who lived by the truths in the Scrolls. Just before giving up and returning home to report of his lack of success, he decided to speak with a seer. He had never believed in their powers, but he was now desperate, and this was his last hope.

He shared his story of his months of frustration while the seer listened intently. When Mahmoud finished his story, the seer finally spoke:

"I can see my friend why you are troubled. But I have an answer to your unspoken question. Yes, there are many merchants who have studied the Scrolls and live by their reason and simplicity. You have been searching in the wrong villages and towns. You will not find them in the cities nor in the caravans."

"Then where will I find them?"

"Patience, Mahmoud. You must use the wisdom contained in the Scrolls to find merchants who have mastered their principles. You have failed to use Scroll number five and six. Can you recite these two Scrolls for me?"

"Scroll number five is about planning. Scroll number six contains wisdom about paying attention."

"And you have done neither in your search. You have not been successful because of your lack of planning prior to your journey. you have been so concerned with yourself and your mission that you have failed to see the signals that were around you every moment of your journey."

"What signals have I missed?"

"That is for you to discover and learn. If I answer your question, you will not learn how to change your ways."

"Am I destined to spend many more months in the desert and unfriendly cities before I learn these lessons?"

"That is up to you, my friend."

"Then my visit with you has been a waste of my time."

"If you say so."

"I want answers. I have been told you give answers to people's questions."

"You have believed the myths about seers if you believe our role is to give answers. Our only purpose is to open doors of thought, and show people what is on the other side. They must decide to pass through. They must be willing to risk, change, believe, and have faith in themselves and their urgings. People need to become more comfortable with where they want to be than with where they are. You must begin your search again from the beginning. You must think clearly, plan carefully, and then follow your path toward your destiny."

"But the king is in a hurry."

"Did he say he was in a hurry?"

"No, but I know him well. I am sure he is anxious for my successful return."

"Would you rather return earlier as a failure or later as a success?"

"Later as a success."

"Then begin again."

He vanished into thin air.

He spent the evening going over in his mind again and again the months of failure trying to discover the signals he had missed. he suddenly realized that he just left the king's presence, and immediately began his search. he had no idea where to look or what to look for. he was certain that he wouldn't have recognized a merchant who knew of, and practiced the wisdom of the Scrolls, if they knocked him over.

He had made the mistake that so many merchants make. He had no clear vision of what he was looking for and where to find it. He just spent his time looking.

He decided the best course of action was a restful night and a new beginning. Prior to retiring to his tent, he penned a letter to the king. he would send it out to him with the caravan that was leaving the city tomorrow. He completed the letter, sealed it, and fell off to sleep.

The morning was filled with a great deal of activity. People were rushing in every direction. Merchants screamed and hustled peasants in the square trying to sell them their wares. Some had greater success than others, so He decided to study the approaches and techniques of the more successful merchants. He observed many throughout the day. Most of the successful merchants seemed to have an endless supply of energy, creativity, and perseverance. They shrugged off the "no's, and they stored their coins from their successful sales with the same enthusiasm and determination. Nothing seemed to daunt these merchants.

One in particular stood out during the day. His robes were clean and his demeanor friendly. He knew his merchandise better than any of the other merchants and He spent time with his customers

He was neither rushed, nor did he rush his customers. he asked many questions before he began his sales appeal, and At the end of the day, when he closed his tent, his purse was overflowing with gold coins.

He approached him and asked if he would join him for dinner. He said he would be honored to be his guest. But that we would need to eat in his home. He said after a full day in the market, he wanted to spend time with his family. I was welcome to join him and his family for the evening.

He accepted. As we walked toward his home, he shared stories about his customers, other merchants who were less successful, and why he believed his purse filled every day while others left the market discouraged, broke, and frustrated. As he listened, he observed the calmness as well as the passion in his voice. He was happy, and he loved selling his wares in the market each day. He never tired of helping people with their problems, needs, and desires.

He had decided to be a merchant years ago when he was a young boy working in his father's tent. His father was one of the most successful merchants in the city, and died a happy and contented man.

"What made you decide to follow in your father's footsteps as a merchant?" mahmoud asked.

"Many years ago my father shared with me the secrets to his success. He took me late one night into his chamber and unrolled copies of the twelve ancient Scrolls that he kept safely locked with his belongings."

This was going to be a very exciting evening. Mahmoud knew finally he was on the right path.

they finished their evening meal and retired to his new friend's study.

"Joseph, please tell me more about your father."

"He was a quiet man and mot a typical merchant. He was kind, understanding, and he accepted people at face value. When a customer said he was unhappy with his purchase for any reason, he would return their money without question. He would then ask them to select one of his other pieces of merchandise at no charge to make up for the inconvenience. People rarely took him up on this offer, but his generosity and understanding spread throughout the kingdom. He prospered even during the dark days of the economic plague. Other merchants had to sell their wares, and even their tents, for a fraction of their value, but my father prospered."

"Why do you believe he was so successful?"

"I asked that very question when I was older."

"And what was his answer?"

"He told me that it was because of the wisdom contained in the twelve Scrolls.

"Mahmoud, are you familiar with the Scrolls?"

"Yes, I have read them."

"have you studied their truths and the wisdom behind their words?"

"Yes, I have studied them, but I am afraid I have much to learn about their true meaning."

Joseph retrieved the Scrolls and they settled in for a long discussion. Mahmoud explained the mission that the king had sent him on. he shared his frustration with joseph caused by his lack of success. Joseph just listened while he told him of his many mistakes and inability to find any of the merchants who understood and applied the truths of the Scrolls. When Mahmoud had finished his story, Joseph suggested that they get some sleep and continue their discussion in the morning. Mahmoud reluctantly agreed and retired to his chamber.

Mahmoud slept very late in the morning. When he entered the dining area, and asked where Joseph was, his wife informed him that he had left hours ago to get an early start in the day. He dressed and finished his breakfast, then left to join Joseph in the market. When he arrived, Joseph's tent was filled with peasants as well as royalty purchasing, and exchanging a variety of goods with Joseph.

"Good morning, Mahmoud." His cheerful voice penetrated through the noise and chatter of the crowd.

"Good morning, Joseph. I see you are having a busy morning."

"Yes, this is the last day of the market, so many of the travelers are purchasing stores for their journeys. Why don't you help me with some of the customers?"

"I would be delighted."

Almost every one of Joseph's customers had purchased from him before. If they were new, it was because someone had recommended his shop over another merchant's. There was a long line of people waiting patiently to exchange their gold coins for Joseph's wares.

At noon we closed the tent for an hour while Joseph and I broke bread together in a nearby cafe. As we ate, Joseph began to share the wisdom of the twelve Scrolls with me.

"Mahmoud, Scroll one reads: *People buy from people they trust.*

"This is the foundation of all success. Many years ago, everyone believed that people bought from those they liked. This myth was passed on from generation to generation. People never questioned its reason. They just continued to try and build relationships based on this theory.

"It wasn't until there were many more merchants selling similar wares, that the old myth began to lose its influence over selling behavior. It is true that people need to respect and like the merchant, but they will not exchange their coins for this reason alone. Trust must be established before people will believe much of the merchant's message. Trust is the foundation for lasting and mutually beneficial customer relationships.

"When trust leaves the relationship, customers will look elsewhere to purchase their goods. Many merchants believe that they must have a lower price in order to sell. What they fail to realize is that when there is a high level of trust, price rarely gets in the way of a successful transaction. when trust is missing in the relationship, even the lowest price will not convince the customer to buy."

"Joseph, how does one establish trust with a potential customer that you have just met?"

"That is a very good question, Mahmoud - one that many merchants never really address in their career. The foundations of trust are built slowly, little by little. In the beginning, a merchant must accomplish this difficult task by doing many little things early in the relationship."

"What are they?"

"First, they must communicate that they care by asking good questions, paying attention, listening well, and taking notes. Next, they must not make promises that they can not keep, or their suppliers cannot keep. Broken promises, even little ones, erode trust. Next, they must have the highest standards of integrity and ethics. They must also look and act in a professional manner at all times. They must know their merchandise, and the merchandise of the other merchants. This is only the beginning. when the relationship is just beginning, it is enough to ensure the customer will be receptive to the merchant's story."

"What is the second Scroll?"

"Mahmoud, you are in too much of a hurry. There is more to the Scrolls than just learning their words or the wisdom behind them. I must return to my tent. Why don't you test the wisdom of the first Scroll? We will meet again here tomorrow for lunch. Good luck."

"Joseph, can you recommend an inn where I can spend the evening?"

"each of the inns in the city has many good points and some bad ones. I will let you select one that you feel is up to your standards. Good bye, Mahmoud, enjoy your day."

Chapter Three

I spent the afternoon in search of a room for the evening. I interviewed many clerks trying to find an inn that would meet my needs. I noticed while I talked with each of the clerks, that none of them seemed to care whether I stayed in their inn. They were too busy with their own chores to spend any time with me. They did answer my many questions, but did not offer any additional information that would help me make my choice. I walked away from each of these inns, not trusting that the information I was given was accurate. Joseph was right. Listening, concern, and interest help establish trust.

I had one more inn to visit. It was the last one in the city and it was located on the edge of the city far from the square. There was a great deal of activity in front of the inn. I entered and approached the clerk. He greeted me with a broad smile and asked how he could help me.

"I am looking for a room for the evening. I may also need it for a few extra days, but I will not know until tomorrow."

"I am sorry sir, but all our rooms are taken. But if you don't mind sharing a room with another traveler, I can ask him if he minds sharing it with you."

"I do not mind."

"Please wait here a moment. I will return shortly."

The clerk was only gone a few minutes. When he returned, he said he had good news.

"The other guest would be happy to share his room with you. He is a very successful caravan leader. He visits here often. I am sure you will like him. Why don't you wait in the courtyard and have something to drink? He will join you shortly. I will bring him out to meet you when he has finished his meeting with his caravan guide."

There was such a difference between this clerk and all the others I had met. He was friendly and genuinely interested in trying to help me with my needs. He went out of his way to be of service. Now I knew why this inn was full and all the others had many vacant rooms.

As I waited in the courtyard, I observed many people introducing themselves to each other. This inn was one of the friendliest I had ever visited. Two elderly merchants came up and asked if they could join me.

"Please sit down. My name is Mahmoud, I am from King Harold's kingdom in the east."

"We have heard of him. We knew his father many years ago. Why are you in this city, Mahmoud?"

"I am searching for merchants who....."

"Say no more. We too, are on a mission to discover the Ancient scrolls."

"Then you have you heard of them?"

"Yes, people in our city are tired of doing business with merchants that do not practice the wisdom that is contained in them. We are here to locate the source of their success for all these many years."

The clerk arrived and said, "Mahmoud, I would like you to meet Haroun, he will be sharing his room with you this evening."

"Hello Haroun, my name is Mahmoud. I wish to thank you for your willingness to share your room with me. There are no other rooms in the inn this evening."

"Mahmoud, it is my pleasure. I, too, have been in your situation. I must go now. I have much preparation to make before our caravan will be ready to depart. Will you join me for the evening meal?"

"I would be delighted."

"Very well, I will meet you here in the courtyard when the sun sets. There will be three others joining us as well."

One of the elderly gentlemen who had joined me asked if that was Haroun, the Caravan leader from the northern kingdom.

"I do not know, I just met him. But, why do you ask?"

"I believe he is the one we came here to find. He has a reputation of being one of the most successful caravan leaders in the entire country. Would you mind if we join you for dinner?"

"It would be my pleasure. I am sure Haroun will not mind."

"Thank you my friend, we will see you later."

The sun was about to dip below the horizon when I saw Joseph coming my way.

"Hello Mahmoud, how was your afternoon?"

"Quite interesting. I met a caravan leader from the north, by the name of haroun who said he would share his room with me. I also met two travelers who knew Harold's father and are also looking for the Scrolls. The caravan leader asked me if I would join him for dinner. He also said that there would be three other people joining us. I gladly accepted. Are you eating alone or would you like to join us?"

"Thank you Mahmoud, but I am one of the three of which he spoke."

"But there is something very curious. When I met Haroun, I was sitting with two elderly gentlemen. I did not introduce them to him before he left.

"The two travelers asked me if they could also join us. They believe the caravan leader is the one they are searching for, who can help them find the scrolls. They did not appear to know him, so how did he know that these two gentlemen would be joining us?"

"I don't know, here comes Haroun now, let's ask him."

Chapter Four

"Good evening gentleman. Welcome. Thank you all for joining me.

"It is not a coincidence that we are all here together this evening. First, let me introduce everyone. This is Joseph, he is a merchant here in this city. This is Mahmoud, he has come a great distance in search of merchants who have mastered the wisdom of the Scrolls. This is Khatib, he is the council leader from Askar, and traveling with him is Ahmed, his friend and companion. They are also searching for the wisdom behind the Scrolls. Now that we are all acquainted, let us order some wine to celebrate this occasion."

"Haroun," I asked, "how did you know Khatib and ahmed would be joining us?"

"what occasion are we celebrating?" Ahmed asked.

Haroun responded, "I will share all, in time. Please no questions now. Let us share a meal, and learn of each other's interest in the Scrolls."

We talked well into the evening. A cool breeze filled the air as we shared the experiences that brought us to this special meeting. After everyone had their turn, and the meal was complete, Haroun suggested we retire to his chamber. There was something he wanted to show us. Several minutes later, we entered his room and sat in a circle. In the center was an old brown worn trunk.

Haroun spoke. "My friends there is something I would like to show you. But first I must warn you. What you are about to witness will change the course of history.

" For many years, the Ancient Scrolls were thought to be the foundation of business and personal success. Many people have searched for the scrolls, and many have believed in their wisdom without ever having seen them personally. What you are about to see are the original twelve Scrolls. They were discovered recently by a priest who decided that he should pass them on to me."

"How do you know they are the originals?"

"Because there are twenty-four Scrolls. For centuries, it was believed that there were only twelve. People were satisfied with the truths that the twelve shared. However, many merchants, after learning of the twelve and mastering there truths, believed that there must be others. No one really knew why, or if their were more where they would be found. The priest discovered them while excavating for a new church.

"They were buried beneath several large boulders. He had planned to build around the boulders, but one of the workmen disturbed one of the rocks and it fell away revealing the end of the trunk. The priest had it removed, opened it, and had it delivered to me."

"Haroun, why have you asked each of us to join you?"

"The world is about to undergo a tremendous change. Business will be conducted in very different ways than it ever has since the beginning of time. There will be new methods of keeping and transmitting information. Business will move much faster than any of us can imagine. All of these changes will require a new set of standards for dealing with people. The old ways will not permit people to live with peace and joy as this new world order comes into being."

"When is all of this going to take place?"

"It is beginning as we speak. The first twelve Scrolls were appropriate for the old-world, but the new Ancient scrolls will require even greater understanding and wisdom. Each of you is familiar with the original twelve. It is my understanding that you know of their wisdom whether you practice them or not. Let us review the original twelve before I share with you the wisdom of the second set of Ancient twelve scrolls."

We spent a few hours discussing the original twelve Scrolls, and their purpose. When we had finished this discussion, Haroun said it was now time to open the trunk, and begin to discuss scrolls thirteen through twenty-four. We waited in silence as he opened the trunk. There was a sense of peace that suddenly filled the room as he removed the carefully wrapped Scrolls. He unrolled Scroll number thirteen and read aloud.

"Scroll number thirteen is about harmony. It shares the message that without harmony in every aspect of our life it is impossible to achieve full and lasting success, and peace in all other areas. Many people over the centuries have attempted to achieve greatness without the knowledge of this Scroll, but their outer successes and achievements have always been marred by an inner lack of peace and joy.

"Please Tell me why you think it is necessary to comprehend, and act upon the wisdom of this thirteenth Scroll."

Ahmed spoke first. "For many years I have always considered myself an outer success, however, any success that I achieved in my younger years was always short-lived. I was always focused on the outer circumstances, rather than the inner growth. As a result, I have often sabotaged myself, if not consciously, then unconsciously. My lack of harmony was the result of the idea that no matter how much I had or accomplished, it would never be enough."

Joseph listened intently as each of the group shared their interpretation and insight into the thirteenth Scroll.

Finally he also spoke. "Gentleman, each of your interpretations is accurate and valuable from where I sit. however, I believe we are all missing the important message in this Scroll."

"And what do you feel that is?" Asked Mahmoud.

Joseph answered, "Harmony is the rule of the universe. Everything since the beginning of time has been in perfect balance. Nature knows only perfect balance. Often some group or individual believes they can outwit this perfect universe by attempting to manipulate or modify the rules to suit their own particular needs or desires. But, in the long run, the universe makes adjustments and brings whatever is out of balance back into harmony. Notice I am using the words balance and harmony interchangeably. One will usually accompany the other. We may often think we are following the rules of nature or the universe, but there is always evidence when we are not. We can choose to ignore the evidence, but that does not change god's grand beautiful plan."

Haroun asked, "Khatib, why do you think harmony is the subject of the thirteenth Scroll?"

"That is difficult to answer because I do not know the Scrolls that follow it. If I knew them I would be better able to give you my opinion."

"Khatib, my friend, that is precisely the type of answer I would have expected from someone who was less informed as to the true nature of the Ancient Scrolls themselves. We must not just look at the Scrolls as only individual parts, but an entire integrated whole. Do not be misled that any Scroll can only stand alone. Please answer my question from that perspective."

"Very well. If, harmony and balance is the rule rather than the exception in nature, whenever any other aspect of any of the Scrolls is out of balance regardless of its nature, it would seem to me that the interpretations of the wisdom of the others would be of little value."

"Khatib, that is a wonderful answer, but does not address the question I asked. Why do you think this concept is the subject of the thirteenth Scroll?"

"I am afraid I do not know, Haroun."

"Mahmoud, what about you?"

"I am afraid I do not know either."

"Does anyone know?"

No one answered.

"Very well, I will give you my answer, but I am disappointed that none of you had either the insight or awareness to answer my question.

"The Thirteenth Scroll is a bridge between the first twelve and the last eleven. It summarizes each of the principles that is necessary for success, and these are described so concisely in Scrolls One through Twelve. It foreshadows the key ingredients that will be found in Scrolls fourteen through Twenty-Four.

"Where the first twelve scrolls are about success, the last twelve are about peace, happiness, satisfaction, and joy. These are the true goals in life, and why people search their entire lives for success, fame, and fortune. But these are like beautiful empty vessels, lovely to gaze upon, but of no real useful value. Oh yes, they might bring beauty to your home and value to your balance sheet, but these are of no use to someone who has a broken heart, lonely existence, or selfish lifestyle.

"To fully benefit from all of the Scrolls, one must master the principles in both the first and last twelve."

Haroun carefully re-tied the thirteenth Scroll and placed it in the trunk. Then he removed the Scroll marked fourteen. We all waited patiently as he unwrapped the colorful cloth ribbon that tightly wound around the Scroll. He read aloud:

"Scroll number fourteen discusses the principle of Joy. It tells us that our joy does not come from our outer environment or experiences, but from our inner acceptance, love of ourselves, and sense of gratitude for where we are, what we are doing, and what we have, regardless of how much or how little. That if we experience more or less joy because of what we have, or what we are doing in our outer world, we will always feel a sense of uneasiness or anxiety due to the temporary, and un-fulfilling nature of these conditions or circumstances. Joy is not about having, doing, or achieving; it is about being. It is living life from the inside-out, not the outside-in."

"But Haroun, many of the merchants and leaders in our cities seem to be very happy with their lives which are filled with possessions and high position."

"Mahmoud, the Scrolls tell us not to be fooled by outer appearances. Many of these people are slaves to their possessions and positions. They put their trust and security in them, as if they will be there for the rest of their lives. Have you ever known anyone who had much and was happy, and upon losing it all lost their sense of meaning and purpose in life?"

"Yes, I do know of many such people. But isn't it possible to have much and still live with an inner sense of joy?"

"Yes, there are many such people in our city and the cities beyond the horizon, but they have a peaceful coexistence with their power, fame, and fortune. If they were to lose it all, they would not lose their joy. It comes from an inner knowing that all is well, and will be well no matter what appearance their outer circumstances or lives may take."

"Haroun, why do you believe this Scroll is included? What is its relationship to being successful as a merchant?"

"Let us ask Joseph for his answer to your question. Joseph?"

"In my early years as a new merchant, I knew little. I was not aware of the wisdom in the Scrolls. Everyday seemed to be filled with yet another struggle. I would get up early in the morning, open my shop, and end the day without a single transaction. My purse was empty, my mind was filled with anger, and my heart with sadness and fear. One day I met a traveling merchant from a far-a-way land in the west. He approached my shop and observed as people were passing by.

He entered and asked to speak with the owner. I told him that I was the owner and asked him how I could help him. He responded by saying that he was here to help me.

"We talked for several minutes and he left without purchasing any of my merchandise."

""Joseph, what did he say to you?"

"He told me that it was obvious from my facial expression and posture that I was not having a very good day. In addition, he said that he believed I was not very happy with my chosen profession as a merchant, and that I might consider some other career."

"That seems a rather bold and arrogant thing to say to a total stranger after only observing him for a few moments."

"That is the strange part. He said he had visited my shop on many earlier occasions, but never purchased anything."

"Did you remember him?"

"No."

Haroun finally spoke, "what did you learn from his visit?"

"I learned that I could not cover my inner fear, anger, frustration, and anxiety. That as much as I thought I was not letting all of this show, it was obviously being expressed without my conscious permission. I also learned that my lack of inner joy was getting in the way of my success.

"I was letting my past poor performance and lack of success sabotage my future success by bringing all of my negative feelings, especially my lack of joy, to each new encounter with each new customer. Some may have wanted the merchandise I had for sale, but they didn't buy. I discovered from this merchant that people like to buy from people who love what they are doing whether they are successful or not. They are grateful for the privilege to be able to help their customers have a better way of life as a result of the purchase of their wares.

"My focus was on my lack and what I was not receiving, and not on the joy of service and giving. Once I realized that my outer circumstances were a reflection of my overwhelming inner feelings of foreboding and discouragement, I was able to re-focus myself."

It was Khatib who asked, "How did this new awareness change your life?"

"From that moment on, my life was never the same. Business improved instantly. Every day My shop was filled with customers who not only were happy to visit with me, but purchased many items as well. I have had some bad times in business since then, but I have never lost my sense of joy for the opportunity to learn, grow, and serve. I am convinced that my business improved and eventually prospered not because of the times, circumstances, or merchandise I carried, but because of my outlook."

Haroun interrupted, "Joseph, you have shared a valuable story with each of us on the purpose of this Scroll. I do not believe we need further discussion. Gentleman, let's look at the next Scroll."

Just as Haroun began to unroll the fifteenth Scroll, there was a knock on the door. He quickly replaced the Scroll in the trunk and closed the lid. He went to the door, opened it and gasped.

"This can't be, I was informed that you had met an ill fate years ago." Haroun said with amazement as he and the stranger embraced and whispered to each other.

Haroun turned and spoke to us, "Kahlil has been traveling for many days and he is in need of nourishment. Please excuse us for a few moments."

As they left the chamber, Haroun asked, "why are you here, Kahlil?"

"You will know soon, my old friend."

Chapter Five

After a few minutes, Haroun returned and announced that his friend was weary and in need of rest. "He would like to join us when we resume our discussion of the Scrolls tomorrow. It is late. Why don't we adjourn for the day? Can you all meet here at noon tomorrow?"

Everyone nodded that they would.

As we were leaving, Ahmed asked me if I would join Khatib and him for a glass of wine.

I said I would join them shortly.

I entered the cafe and found Khatib and Ahmed seated at a table in the far left corner. They waved for me to join them. I sat and joined them.

The late evening discussion was light and friendly. We didn't discuss the events and conversation of the evening in Haroun's chamber. Khatib and Ahmed had been friends for many years. They had spent the last several years traveling together from city to city to find evidence of the Scrolls.

They all felt fortunate to be included in the little group that was discussing the wisdom of the Scrolls. They were searching for the Scrolls, that was true, but it was not an emotional crusade. Somehow, they knew that if they trusted the universe, it would eventually guide them to the place where their journey would come to a successful end.

We said good night and parted.

As I walked back to the inn, I couldn't help but notice an elderly woman who seemed to be following me. I stopped and rested for few minutes to see if she would pass on by, but she approached me and asked me if I could spare a few coins. I gave her all I had. She was very grateful. She then slowly walked off with tears in her eyes.

She reminded me of the time when I was in desperate need of a kind word and support. I Hadn't yet met the king, and I was living on the outskirts of the city in a shabby tent that let in both the light and the dust from the desert. In the evenings, the desert can be very cold and unfriendly. I survived those many years of hardship because I knew one day my desire to succeed would overtake my poor conditions.

One day the king was riding through the desert in search of peasants who wanted to serve him in his castle. I didn't know he was the king. I had never met or seen him. He traveled without the adornments of his position. I believe he did this for reasons of safety rather than humility. He stopped at my tent and asked if I knew any peasants who were hard working and pleasant. I asked him what his purpose was in asking.

"I may have several positions available in the city in the near future. I am only gathering names at this time."

I gave him the names of several I thought might meet his needs and mischievously included mine in the list. I didn't hear from the king for several months and just assumed he had some other reason for asking, or that he had contacted everyone on the list but me. One day, one of his special guards approached my tent and asked if I would join him on a trip to the city to visit with the king. I asked him what the king wanted to see me about, but he just asked me once again if I would join him.

As I entered the king's inner chamber, I was afraid and nervous. My clothes were rags and I was covered with the dirt from a day's toil in my garden. The king was friendly and warm. He asked me to join him for lunch. During our meal, he told me about his vision to build a new city with shops filled with wonderful merchandise being sold by friendly and knowledgeable merchants. I listened with great interest, wondering why he was taking his time to tell me this story.

He concluded by asking if I would become one of his inner circle of advisors in the project. I told him I had no experience, but he would not be put off.

"But why me, sire?"

"One day you will know, my friend."

After much discussion, I finally accepted the position wondering what my new role would be, and where it would lead me.

I never thought several years ago while working in my garden, a broken and discouraged man, that I would one day be seated in the chamber with a group of a very wise men many miles away in a strange new city.

I reached the inn and went in and settled down for a night's sleep. Tomorrow would be another very interesting day, I was sure.

Joseph woke me at dawn to tell me he was going to his shop and would meet me back here at the inn at Haroun's chamber at noon. After he left, I arose and washed before taking my morning meal.

Chapter Six

Everyone was on time. Haroun introduced Kahlil to
everyone as he joined us in the chamber. He said that
Kahlil would be able to add some interesting insight to
our discussion.

Kahlil began, "Years ago I left the city in search of
success, wealth and happiness. The more I looked
outward the more I realized that all of these lie within.
This lesson fortunately came with a great deal of pain
and sacrifice."

Joseph interrupted, "Kahlil, your last statement seems a little strange.

"I will explain, but first I must tell you what led up to these lessons. I had been gone several years when I met a man who would later become a valuable friend and mentor. He was much younger than me so needless to say I was skeptical of his ability to teach me. During the early days of our relationship I learned many things about life, success and the search for love and happiness. It wasn't until he passed away at a very early age that I discovered how much his wisdom had increased my own. I miss his friendship and counsel a great deal, but life has a way of teaching us all, even in death.

Prior to his passing we had been sharing a meal at his home. He lived in very humble circumstances so I always assumed that he was not a rich man. Later I discovered that his wealth was vast and he willingly shared it with those less fortunate. In his giving he received much. He left me more than gold, he left me with many memories and much insight, insight that I know was worth more than any riches he could have left me. When I returned from my travels to visit my young friend his wife gave me an envelope which contained instructions to return to the city and join you in your discussions. I had no idea what he was referring to so I placed the envelop with my other belongings and forgot about it until one day months later when I was attacked by a band of robbers while on my way to visit my daughter and her family.

The robbers took all of my possessions and left me to die in the hot desert sun. Fortunately I was rescued by a caravan on its way to the city. Along the way we spotted some of my belongings on the side of the road. They had taken all of my valuable possessions but left the envelope. I can only guess that they couldn't read or that they saw no value in it. When I read the instructions one more I had this sudden sense of urgency to follow its instructions. He briefly mentions the Scrolls and asked if I would participate in the discussion on their truth and merits. Not knowing what he was talking about I decided to leave the caravan and return to see his wife to see if she could explain what he meant by the message.

When I returned, I discovered that his wife and two children had disappeared. I was curious to see why. So I asked several of his friends and none could be of any help. It seems that she just vanished one morning without a trace.

There seems to be a great deal of mystery surround all of these events. His sudden death of an unknown cause, his wife's departure and the strange instructions. Everywhere I turned for help there were more questions than answers until one evening I had a vision of my friend standing in my room. He had warm smile and calm demeanor as he tried to get my attention. Joseph, I have never believed in 'the other side' the way so many mystics have described through the years. Yes, I believe in God and his ultimate power but I just never could accept the reality of, I am not sure how to put this, Angels or messengers to everyday people. He asked my way I had not yet left to visit you in the city to discuss the Scrolls.

I could not answer. I felt like I was looking right through him. He patiently asked again and waited for me to respond. I finally told him I did not have a good reason for waiting."

He began, "Kahlil, wisdom and knowledge are important for success. Patience and persistence are also valuable traits. And commitment, study and belief are also worthy, but sooner or later each of us must act, often acting on faith and faith alone. None of us can know what lies ahead. We can not know the consequences of our decisions, actions and choices. And, this is good. But there are always lessons in all decisions and actions whether positive or negative. Waiting is a useless waste of time. You are here only a short time. To wait is to ensure failure. To act is to not guarantee success, but it is better to fail while acting than fail by waiting.

I know you my old friend. You want answers. You have searched for them all of your days. But, Kahlil there are no answers only more questions as we travel the path of life. Some answers seem unfair, like my untimely death and the disappearance of my family. You have searched for years to find happiness, love and peace. You have traveled far to discover the secrets of success. I left you with a gift, the opportunity to find what you were searching for but you lacked faith in my instructions. Why? Because you lack understanding of what faith really is.

Faith is knowing without seeing. It is believing without knowing. It is understanding and accepting without believing and it is trust in the face of discouragement, despair and failure. People who have faith are often described like the village idiot. They are seen as hopeless romantics and positive believers without evidence. Kahlil, life seldom gives us evidence in the present but it always gives it to us in the past. Faith is your answer to all of your searching. You must learn to have faith."

"But......"

"Please let me finish, my time with you is very brief. When you arrive at Joseph's, please give him a message for me. I have not seen him since he was a child but our fathers were very good friends. He will remember me, I guarantee just tell him that Shadon sends his love, peace and best wishes to him and his family. Although we have not kept in contact all these years I have learned of his success as a merchant. His reputation, like his fathers is known throughout the Kingdom. Please tell him that he must complete his discussions of the Scrolls before it is too late. Now, my old friend it is time for me to leave you. Go about your business and join the search for the meaning of the Scrolls. And when you have completed your journey take what you have learned and share it with the world. Kahlil, stop your searching and begin your sharing. Good bye, I will see you in another place where we will all live in harmony, peace and love."

His presence just disappeared, vanished before I could ask him even one question."

Joseph asked, "what would you have asked him my friend?"

"I don't really know. There were so many questions."

Haroun now spoke, "That is an interesting story Kahlil but I believe we should resume our discussions. shall we begin where we left off, with Scroll fifteen?"

Everyone smiled and nodded in wholehearted agreement.

Haroun began, *"Scroll number fifteen talks of patience. It tells us that what we achieve that is lasting and worthwhile comes only after we have waited. It does not mean to imply that we sit idly by just waiting for our good to come to us. It makes very clear that we must do our part, but it also stresses that while we are doing our part we must not attempt to change the rules and time table of the universe.*

What you sew, you will one day reap.

"Sew anger and hatred, and one day you will reap sickness and a broken spirit. Sew bad thoughts, and one day you will reap a troublesome mind. Sew arrogance and rudeness, and one day you will reap scorn and ridicule. Sew a lack of discipline and purpose, and one day you will reap aimlessness and failure. Sew jealousy and envy, and one day you will reap frustration and endless longing. Sew resentment and blame, and one day you will reap hostility and spite. Sew greed and lust, and one day reap loneliness and emptiness. Sew laziness and sloppiness, and one day you will reap poverty and a shabby environment.

It states further, *"that when you sew love, you reap peace. Sew kindness, and reap compassion. Sew diligence, and reap patience. Sew faith, and reap* understanding. *Sew knowledge, and reap wisdom. Sew compassion, and reap a soft demeanor. Sew trust, and reap calmness. Sew honesty, and reap a worry free mind. Sew good thoughts, and reap good results. Sew generosity, and reap hospitality. Sew effort, and you will reap satisfaction. Sew purpose, and reap success."*

"Gentlemen, what are your thoughts on the fifteenth Scroll, patience?"

Joseph was first to speak, "Haroun, I am not sure I understand the relationship between patience, the theme of the Scroll, and the discussion on sewing and reaping."

"Mahmoud, what are your thoughts on Joseph's question?"

"It reminds me of a time in my life when I wanted much, but had little. I had a choice to focus on what I did not have, while hoping that one day I would achieve fame, power, and wealth. even though I was surrounded by lack, I could envision and work toward that which one day I imagined would be my surroundings. Therefore, I had to rise above my present circumstances, if not in deed, then in thought, and work toward those circumstances that would one day be, rather than the ones that were present. This task was not an easy one.

"I was surrounded by people who would question my positive attitude and work habits in the midst of poverty. They would call me a hypocrite and dreamer. They would call me insane and useless. It required much inner courage to ignore these constant messages form my outer world and stay focused on the dreams, desires, and positive outcomes I knew one day would be mine.

"So day after day, I sewed good thoughts, actions, and beliefs. I sit here today, several years later with this prestigious circle, , as a testimony to this process. It is not by accident or wishing that I have arrived in your presence, but by the patient sewing of right actions, emotions and beliefs."

"Mahmoud, that is a wonderful example. It clearly puts the message of the fifteenth Scroll in perspective. Are there any other comments or questions about this Scroll?"

Khatib asked, "Mahmoud, how were you able to keep on indefinitely with your positive outlook while all around you was powerful evidence that you were not making progress?"

"Khatib, my friend, we can not judge the circumstances of our future by the appearance of the present. To do so is to live without hope and any positive expectancy. I knew deep inside that It was right to dream, and desire a better way of life. I also knew that focusing on my present conditions would only bring more of them into my life."

"Mahmoud, you have still not told me how you did it."

It was Ahmed who came to Mahmoud's rescue.

"Khatib, there is only one thing that a person can do in the present to change his future, and that is to use the power of the mind to imagine. We can choose to imagine positive or negative, good or evil, happiness or sadness, success or failure. The mind is a tool that must be used. When our imagination and thoughts are not controlled, they will fall prey to every negative word, picture, and feeling that comes to us from our environment.

"We must learn to prevent these destructive thoughts from entering our mind and let in only those that support our dreams, desires and goals. We do this with our focus. When a negative comment is thrown at us by some well-meaning person, we must filter it, and only let in those that contribute to our objective. When a negative experience finds its way into our life, we must see it as a neutral teacher. We can choose to learn from it, or complain and bemoan our stock in life with such reactions as - why me, life isn't fair, I don't deserve this, and so on. We must guard the entry to our mind with determination. We must fill our mind each moment with what can be, not what is."

"May we move on to the next Scroll, or do we need more discussion of this Scroll about patience?"

It was Khatib who spoke next. "I accept and believe all I have heard. But, I still need further explanation about patience. Would someone give me their interpretation or definition of patience from the Scroll's perspective?"

Haroun seemed anxious to move on, feeling that Khatib should know the answer to his question, but he gave the following explanation. "Khatib, each of us has a different perspective on time. Time moves slowly when we are bored, and quickly when we are enjoying ourselves. in reality time never speeds up or slows down; it just is perceived by each of us as doing so. Patience is trust and faith in action. It is the demonstration of acceptance with what is now. It is also believing that what will be in the future will be better or different, regardless whether that future is in five minutes, or twenty years. It is living in the present moments of your life. It is desiring that what we want will come into our lives, but if it doesn't come on our schedule or ever, that is acceptable. It is a peaceful partnership with the flow and unfolding of your life."

"Thank you Haroun, it is very clear to me now."

"Let us take a refreshment break."

As we were beginning to leave Haroun's room, Kahlil finally spoke. His silence was very noticeable during the entire discussion. "

"When we return, I have a story to tell you that will end any doubts in your mind about the wisdom of the scrolls."

"Thank you Haroun, it is very clear to me now."

"Let us take a refreshment break."

As we were beginning to leave Haroun's room, Kahlil finally spoke. His silence was very noticeable during the entire discussion. "

"When we return, I have a story to tell you that will end any doubts in your mind about the wisdom of the scrolls."

Chapter Seven

Kahlil began. "Many years ago there was a camel driver by the name of Samile. He was not a popular man or a successful camel driver. He wanted to discover the keys to his lack of success and happiness. One day he left his caravan in the hands of his able assistant, and traveled for many years in search of understanding and awareness. He never found the Answers for which he was searching. Therefore, he gave up and spent the remainder of his life in seclusion. When he was an old man and very close to death, he had a dream. In his dream, He saw twenty-four blank Scrolls, and was told to awake, take a marker, and write on the Scrolls that were next to his bed on the floor. When he first went to sleep there were no Scrolls anywhere in his tent. He reached down beside his bed and picked up one Scroll at a time and wrote as he was instructed. Just after completing the final Scroll, he left this world for the next.

"two trunks containing the Scrolls were found by a passing traveler who buried Samile in his final resting place. The traveler kept the trunks with him for many years. He read the scrolls, but knew not of their purpose. One day in his travels he passed a broken down old church. He left the trunks with the church elder who was in charge of church. The elder did not open the trunks and read the Scrolls, but placed one of the trunks in a hiding place beneath the altar. He placed the second trunk in the basement behind several large boulders. Many years passed. The elder also passed on-never telling anyone about both trunks. One day a band of thieves searched the church for coins and gems. They found none, but did take the trunk they found under the altar.

"The Scrolls eventually found their way to the marketplace and were sold for a few coins to a merchant. The merchant read the Scrolls and put their messages into practice and became very wealthy. But his wealth never made him happy or gave him peace. The wisdom of the twelve original discovered Scrolls quickly spread throughout the land. However, there was always something strange about the original twelve Scrolls. They were written with blue letters, long before the color blue was discovered. If you will notice, the second twelve Scrolls are also written in blue. This mystery has never been given an adequate explanation. This will bring each of you up to date on the history, as we know it, about the twenty-four Scrolls. Would anyone like to comment about this question?"

No one spoke. Each of us looked at the others with a blank stare. Even Haroun was silent. There were several minutes of silence which were finally broken by Ahmed.

"I have heard that story just as our friend Kahlil tells it with one exception. The Scrolls were written in red, the color of blood. But once they were read, they turned to blue. A very strange occurrence, one that none of the seers or mystics have been able to explain."

"Thank you Ahmed, I too had heard that version, but since I had no proof, I left it out of my story."

It was Haroun that broke the silence, "It is obvious that none of us can explain this strange mystery, therefore, Let us leave it for now, and move on to the sixteenth Scroll."

"Joseph why don't you read the next Scroll."

"Very well."

Joseph slowly untied the ribbon holding the Scroll and unrolled it with care. He began to read, "This Scroll is about acceptance. It states that acceptance eliminates the need for all judgment, criticism, blame, resentment, and guilt. Self-acceptance is the key to happiness and inner peace. *Acceptance of others is the highest form of love you can show them. When we judge another, we define ourselves. When we are unable to accept another, it is an expression of our lack of self-acceptance. When we are unwilling to accept ourselves for who and what we are, we will live with anxiety, stress, frustration, and disappointment."*

"Who would like to begin the discussion of the sixteenth Scroll?" asked Haroun. But as he finished his question, one of the servants announced that we had a visitor. We were not expecting anyone, so Haroun asked the servant to ask the stranger his business.

"Sir," the servant said, "it is a woman who calls herself Aziza. She said she was told by her caravan leader to join our group discussing the second set of Scrolls."

"How could she? no one knows about the second set except those of us in this chamber. Have any of you told anyone about our meetings?"

Everyone said, no.

"Then how could the caravan leader and now this woman know?"

Joseph suggested that we let the woman enter and find out.

She was quite beautiful with intelligent penetrating blue eyes, long silky yellow hair, and a white complexion.

She introduced herself to our group by saying that she was told to join us by the caravan leader who was passing through the city, and to deliver a message.

"And what is the message?" asked Haroun.

"That your time is running out. You must complete your interpretation of the second set of Scrolls quickly, and then embark on your separate ways to share the wisdom of the final twelve with the world."

"Why is our time running out?" I asked.

"I do not know. I am only delivering the message."

It was Joseph who surprised us all by asking the woman Aziza to join our group. No one seemed to object.

She accepted and took a seat in the circle surrounding the trunk.

Haroun asked her if she knew of the wisdom from the first set of Scrolls.

She said she knew of them briefly, but had never studied them in detail.

Kahlil suggested that we adjourn for the day and meet again tomorrow morning after sunrise. We all agreed, and left haroun's chamber and walked outside into the bright hot sun. It was mid afternoon. Joseph left to check on his shop. Ahmed and Khatib said they also had some business that needed attention. Kahlil and Haroun stayed behind, and Aziza and I left to find her a room in the city.

Chapter Eight

I awoke early the next morning filled with anxiety and dread. I did not know why, but I believe it was related to the woman's message that time was running out. What did it mean? I had little time to contemplate it as there was a commotion out in the square adjacent to Joseph's home.

I went outside to discover that Aziza was the cause of whatever was happening. She was being detained by several bandits. I approached and asked their business. They told me she was the daughter of one of the most successful merchants in a city four day's ride to the east. They were going to collect a ransom for her from the merchant.

I asked them what ransom they were going to ask for, and they said one hundred gold coins. I told them they had a choice. Accept five gold coins now and release the woman, or leave with neither the woman or the coins. They all laughed, asking how I was going to stop them. I told them they would find out if they were interested. I waited. They looked me up and down curiously. Several minutes passed. I waited. The leader approached me and asked why I would buy this woman. I told him I was not buying her, but setting her free from their evil mission, and that if he was wise he would abandon his mission before it was too late.

"Sir," he said, "I do not believe alone that you can stop the four of us."

"I have no intention of acting alone. Release the woman now, or I will withdraw my offer of the five coins."

"She is yours. She is not worth any more of our trouble." With that, the four men rode off on their camels into the morning sun with their small prize.

"Thank you, Mahmoud. That was kind and brave of you. But I must ask, were you bluffing, or were you counting on help from somewhere?"

"I have seen that group before. They are all talk and no action. I knew they would not want to fight. They did not recognize me, but we had a similar run-in several months ago. Let us get something to eat before we join the others."

When we arrived at Haroun's chamber, where the others were already seated waiting for us, We greeted each other, and made ourselves comfortable.

"Mahmoud, why don't you resume where we left off yesterday by re-reading the sixteenth Scroll."

I did as Haroun asked. When I was finished we spent a great deal of time discussing the message this Scroll offers, that of acceptance. We concluded that acceptance was the foundation of love, brotherhood, success, peace, and inner harmony. Many people lack the ability to accept others, and therefore spend their lives in judgment of others and themselves.

Haroun began to untie the seventeenth Scroll, and then read aloud, *"this Scroll tells us of forgiveness. It says that forgiveness is not about condoning other people's actions or behavior, but its purpose is to release us from the negative emotional hold that it has on our life. People who are unable to forgive others carry a heavy burden in their life. It goes on to state that forgiveness is a healing force and contributes to our peace, inner harmony, and balance."*

Mahmoud asked, "why is forgiveness one of the Scrolls? I thought that these Scrolls' focus was on how to be an effective merchant in the marketplace?"

Joseph responded, "Mahmoud, are you not yet aware that selling is not just about selling merchandise? It is about our ability to influence and persuade others. Many people feel because they do not sell a product or service, that they are not selling. What about the senators in the hall of justice? And the religious leaders who convey the truth about God and spirit? And don't forget all the mothers and fathers who sell values, morals and right thinking to their children. the teachers, lawyers, and Even the beggars on the street are selling."

"What do the beggars sell, Joseph?"

"They are selling a roof over their heads to find shelter from the wind and cold. They are selling their hopes for a few morsels of food so they can survive another day."

Haroun spoke, "Gentlemen and Lady, we are getting off the track. Please, our time is limited, let's stay with the topic of the Scroll at hand. What is your interpretation of forgiveness?"

It was Aziza who now spoke. We waited, as she was a new addition to our group, and we were all anxious for her comments.

"It is difficult for people to forgive others the wrong that is done to them. These people often see other person's acts as specific acts against them. Most people do not deliberately cause harm to others. Yes, it is true that there are a few peasants and nobility who from time to time let their evil nature bring harm and pain to others, but most of the citizens in the cities and beyond are just doing things."

"Aziza, what is the difference in just doing things, or doing things to others"?

"Mahmoud, it is a matter of intent. Few people want to harm or cause pain to their brothers. Their intent is not evil. They may be protecting their ego or emotional stability by acting in such a way that is interpreted by others as behavior that needs forgiveness."

"Can you give us an example?"

"I can. This morning several bandits attempted to abduct me and take me with them for their evil purpose. You interceded on my behalf, and because of timing and your courage, I am able to be with you all this morning. Those men were acting out of fear, greed, the need for power, or their ego drive to return to their village with a yellow haired prize. They acted as they did for reasons that we will never know, and that they may not even be aware. I can carry anger about this incident and their actions with me for many years, but they will not know of my anger. I will, however. And carrying this anger with me will inhibit me from finding peace, joy, and happiness in my life. It will be like a black cloud that I carry into every day of my life. Resenting them, wanting them to be punished, or hoping they meet with a vile ending does not change what happened, and will not allow me to let go and put the incident behind me. I need to forgive their act so that I can move on with peace and love In my heart."

"What if I had not arrived in time, and you found yourself on your way to a terrible fate. Would you still feel forgiveness for them?"

"Mahmoud, you are missing the point of the Scroll. Forgiveness takes place within me. Anger is within me. Resentment is within me. No matter what my outer circumstances, I have the ability, whether I choose to use it, to control my thoughts, emotions and feelings. choosing to not forgive them, captured or otherwise, would have given power over my inner being to those bandits. In the end all we have, each of us, is the control over our private inner world to use for good or harmful outcomes."

"Very well put, Aziza. Does anyone have anything to add?"

Kahlil answered, "Yes Haroun, I would like to offer my interpretation as well. I will do so with a story that took place many years ago.

Kahlil began. "I was just a young man when my parents passed away. They left me with no possessions, nowhere to live, and a great deal of anger and resentment. I was both sad that they had died, and also fearful of how my life would turn out without their support and guidance. I spent many years begging in the streets for food and shelter. There were many times I wanted to give up - not knowing if I would survive another day. I spent many days and nights feeling betrayed and afraid. I had no education, no skills and no living relatives that could assist me. My situation for several years was desperate.

"I am convinced today that the many years I spent angry and lost were due to my holding on to the emotions tied to their passing and leaving me alone in the world. It wasn't until I was finally able to release all of this emotional trauma, anger and resentment through forgiveness that I was able to begin again. One day I went to their grave and spent hours crying and letting go.

"I forgave them for their final act of abandonment. I learned that day that even though my parents were dead, I could still forgive them. I do not know if they are aware of my forgiveness, but I am. When I left their final resting place, I felt a renewed sense of faith, optimism and confidence that I would one day find success and peace. Since that day I have never looked back.

"I have stopped blaming them for my circumstances, and I have learned to love them for what they did give me - life. This gift is the most precious thing anyone can give. Physical life or a renewed emotional and spiritual beginning. Often in my dreams, I see both of my parents smiling at my growth, and what I have become. I am convinced had I not shared that act of forgiveness with them that day, I would still be begging on the streets living a broken and aimless life."

"Kahlil, what prompted you to visit their grave and forgive them?"

"Joseph, I do not know. I was guided quite spontaneously one morning to the site. I didn't go with the intent to forgive, but to lash out in anger one more time. When I arrived, a sense of peace came over me. The anger left and it was replaced with compassion and love, not only for them, but for myself. They were gone, and yet I seemed to be trying to punish them. In the end, I was punishing myself. That day freed me from the hold those negative emotions had over me."

Aziza spoke, "gentlemen, I must remind you our time is running out. we must proceed with the final seven Scrolls quickly."

"Aziza, why is our time running out?"

"Mahmoud, there are forces at work in the universe beyond our understanding that must be listened to even though we can not comprehend their meaning. Man is moving rapidly into a new age, an age where the old myths, principles, and truths will be challenged at every turn. Man needs a new philosophy if he is to survive these many challenges. Our concept of time, history, the future, and the meaning of life itself will need newunderstanding. If we fail to agree on the role the Ancient twelve Scrolls will play in this new order, man is destined to wander in the desert alone, uncertain, and afraid for generations."

"Aziza, are you saying that our discussion of the Scrolls among the six of us is an important one for the future of mankind?"

"Haroun, There are other groups in other cities having similar discussions about the Scrolls, as we speak today."

"But Aziza, these are the original Scrolls. How could other groups be discussing them?"

"I do not have an answer to that question, Haroun my friend. I only know that I was sent a sign from the universe that many groups in distant lands are all looking for the same wisdom. Each group must arrive at its own conclusions separately. But in the end each group, according to my vision, will arrive at the same conclusions. Once that step has been completed, and it could take some groups many more days than others, each group must appoint a leader to take the wisdom and share it with the rest of the people in the world. If that is not accomplished soon, it will be too late and humanity will suffer the consequences of living in darkness for many years."

"Then I suggest we move to the Scroll marked number Eighteen."

"Khatib, you have not yet begun the discussion of a Scroll. Why don't you untie the next Scroll."

"Haroun, I am afraid I can not do so."

Chapter Nine

"And why not Khatib?"

"Because I am blind."

"We did not know. You seem to get along fine without assistance."

"I am not blind in my eyes, but in my spirit. I have looked for many years for wisdom and understanding, and have not discovered the source of my sight. Many people see, but they do not really see. I am one of those people. I see events unfold, and people go through their days and lives, but I have failed to learn from my many lessons the truths that have been presented to me. I have squandered my life in the useless pursuit of recognition, control, riches, and power, but I am without happiness or peace. I lack an understanding mind and a compassionate heart. That is why I have been searching for the Scrolls. I knew that there must have been more than the first twelve. I have mastered their wisdom, and I am still unfulfilled. Life would not, I am convinced, play such an evil trick on man as to give him success and not the power to enjoy or share it. Please let someone else read the next Scroll."

"No Khatib, all discovery is self-discovery, you must read the next Scroll, and give it meaning through the insight of your own experience."

"Very well, please pass me the Scroll."

Khatib began, *"Scroll number eighteen discusses love. It says that love takes many forms: The love of wisdom, the love of one another, the love of self, the love of God, the love of charity, the love of fine wine, the love of our present, the love of our past, the love of health, the love of our children, the love of the present, the love of compassion, the love of work, the love of service, the love of friends, the love of play, the love of truth, the love of humility. It goes on that all love springs from inside the soul of each individual. To refuse to love is to reject ourselves and the love we could share with the world. We must learn to love ourselves unconditionally before we can truly accept the love of others and share open, honest love of anything or anyone with integrity. Where there is no love, there is fear, hopelessness, and discouragement. Where love is present, there is faith, joy, and peace. There is no more."*

"Khatib, will you now give this Scroll meaning in light of your own life?"

"Haroun, I would not know where to begin."

"You are among friends here. It is safe to begin where you feel the most pain, fear, or grief in your heart."

"Very well, When I was growing up, I wanted to please those around me. I sought acceptance and approval from friends, my parents, and many of my teachers. I would often put the needs of others above my own in the hopes that they would give me the recognition I so desperately wanted and needed. I soon learned that no matter how much I did for others, or tried to please them, it was never enough. In the process, I learned to only love myself when I received the acceptance or notice I wanted. My self-love was conditional on doing the right things, thinking the right thoughts, or expressing the right emotions. I became an actor in life in search of applause. It never came. One day I realized that I had done nothing in life up to that point that I wanted to do for me.

"I tried to change, but my behavior was so ingrained that I have been unable to modify it. To this day, I am more concerned with other people's feelings about me than I am with my own feelings about myself. I am tired of putting my own needs and desires second, but I do not know what to do to change. Now I am an old man, and I wonder if it is too late to try any longer."

"Khatib, it is never too late to change. It is true that you cannot change all of the years of disappointment, frustration, and heartache, but you can live all your remaining days with freedom from this emotional bond."

"But how? I have spent many years without success."

"You were unsuccessful because you did not seek counsel. You attempted to change without the guidance or teaching of a tutor, who because of their experience, would have been able to help you break through the inner barriers that stopped you. This is true of so many people who want to change, but lack the knowledge or skill of how to accomplish it. Therefore they experience failure and discouragement. To change requires the awareness that something needs to change, the will to do so, the knowledge of what and how to change, and the desire to put action and commitment to your words.

"When you have all of these, there is only one step remaining - action. The awareness to change comes from your inner frustration with the way things are in your life. The will also comes from within. The knowledge often must come from outside of your experience and awareness from a teacher or guide. The desire and action also come from within. before a teacher can help you see to the other side, you must reach that point in your life when you are ready. We can only guess that all through these years you were not ready yet for the new you. I believe now you are.

"The Scrolls can be a teacher, but they are not the only teacher. You must learn to listen to your inner teacher or knower. It has awareness that you cannot imagine. The Scrolls can only open the doors. you must walk through them yourself. You must become more comfortable with where you want to be than where you are."

"May I offer a suggestion?" Aziza asked.

"Of course."

"Khatib, please answer a question for me. Do you like yourself?"

"Some parts."

"Which parts don't you like?"

"I don't like my weaknesses."

"And what is one you do not like?"

"There are times I don't do what I know I should and other times when I do that which I know I shouldn't. I do not know why I am weak like this, and I despise it in myself."

"What things do you like about yourself?"

"I like my generosity, thoughtfulness, and interest in others."

"Are there times when you don't do for others what you would like?"

"Not very often."

"So the person that generally gets shortchanged the most in your life is you, is that correct?"

"Yes it is."

"There is an old saying: 'what you continually focus on - you will get more of in your life.' What have you been focusing on in your life? the recognition you were getting or that which was lacking?"

"That which was lacking."

"so by focusing in life on your lack of approval or acceptance, would you agree that you have brought even more of this lack into your life?"

"Aziza, I believe you are right. But what can I do about it at this late time in my life?"

"Begin to focus only on that which you are receiving, and ignore that which you are not receiving. Do not give what you are not getting any more of your energy. Only give energy to that which you have. Focus on the love you do have. Focus only on the love you are receiving. No longer focus on the love that you do not receive. Whenever any of these lack thoughts enter your mind, begin to think of someone or something that has been loving to you. Begin to think of someone you can share love with. Do not give these lack thoughts any more room in your mind, and you will discover that before you know it, you will have achieved the control and position you have desired."

"Would anyone else like to comment on the eighteenth Scroll - love?"

Ahmed added, "I would only like to reinforce what Aziza has just shared with Khatib. I, too, have longed for love, but it wasn't until I learned to love myself that the love of others finally came to me. If I withheld love, and only gave it after which I received it, what I got in return was not love, but scorn. We need to love not because the other person or thing deserves it, but because we deserve to give it. And with the giving we increase our love of ourselves. Love is not about the other person, it is about expressing who we are regardless of whether the other person accepts our gift of love. If they reject our gift because they do not feel worthy of it, that is where their growth and learning must be. The message of the Scroll is simple. Our role is to love others whether they want it, deserve it, earn it, or accept it."

"Thank you, Ahmed."

"Let us have our noon day meal. We can resume our discussion after breaking bread together."

I though back on Harold's last words, "when you have discovered merchants who have lived by the Scrolls, bring them to me I have a mission for you to undertake." I wondered if Harold's mission was the one Aziza had spoken of.

We were about to have a surprise guest that would give me a clue to the answer. My thoughts were interrupted by the servant bringing the meal.

Chapter Ten

Our meal conversation was light and joyful. Different circumstances brought each of us to this place, but we were all here for one purpose: to discover how to interpret the Scrolls, apply their wisdom in our lives, and share this wisdom with the world.

We completed our meal, and as the servant was leaving, he announced that we had a visitor.

"Show him in" Haroun said.

"Good day to you all."

I couldn't believe my eyes.

"It has been so many years. Where have you been? How have you been? What brings you to this city? This house?"

"So many questions, Mahmoud my friend. Please introduce me to your guests."

"I would like you all to meet Safia. She is the daughter of an old and dear friend. Safia, this is Joseph a local merchant, Aziza who represents a caravan leader in this part of the world, Ahmed and Khatib who are on a mission to locate the Ancient Scrolls, and Haroun our host."

It was Joseph who spoke next. "What brings you to our city and this meeting?"

"I was sent by my father to find Mahmoud. He recently died, and in his final words he asked me to find you and share the truths of the ancient Scrolls with you."

"We are in the process of discussing them at this time, for each of us has his or her special interest in them" Said Haroun.

Safia continued. "My father shared the wisdom of the Scrolls with me before he died. May I join you?"

"Of course" we all said in unison.

Safia took a seat next to me and we resumed our discussion.

Joseph opened the discussion by reminding us that we were discussing the Eighteenth Scroll, Love.

"Do we need to spend further time on this most important Scroll, or can we move on to Scroll Nineteen?"

Safia spoke. "I do not expect you to repeat your entire discussion of the previous Scrolls for me. could someone summarize for me the meaning of the last one you discussed?"

"Let me try," said Aziza. "Love is the only true emotion in the world. Every other emotion is a degree of love, or the lack of love. Anger and hatred is love withheld. Fear is the lack of self-love. Guilt, blame, and resentment are all emotions that lack love to some degree, While joy, faith, passion, and hope are all positive expressions of love. The world was created in love. The world, whether your personal world or the world around you, works effortlessly when you express your true love nature, and it is filled with stress, anxiety, mistrust and confusion when you withhold your true love nature. Love can not be used up. Share it, and you still have more to share. Receive it, and you can still receive more. Love is not a commodity to be bartered or used for some manipulated goal or outcome. It is a neutral concept that can be shared or withheld, received or rejected."

"Excellent, Aziza. Let us now proceed to Scroll Nineteen. Joseph, will you unwrap and read this next Scroll for us?"

"Certainly, Haroun."

Joseph carefully unwrapped the Scroll and began to read. *"The message in Scroll Nineteen is service to others. It states that service is the highest form of love expressed to others in the world. Service, when rendered without an interest in what will be returned to the giver, will always lead to improved relationships, satisfied customers, and a sense of peace within the giver. However, it goes on to clearly state that service when given with a motive for some return, will always lead to frustration and disappointment for all parties."*

"Thank you Joseph. Now can someone share an example with us that explains the deeper meaning in this Scroll?"

The room was silent. Each of us looked at the others waiting for someone to respond. No one spoke. Just then we noticed the servant had entered the room during the discussion.

The servant asked, "would anyone like a cool beverage?"

After everyone had told the servant what he or she wished, he began to leave the room.

Safia spoke to the servant, and asked him if he would share with us his interpretation of this important Scroll that he had just overheard.

The servant began, "I am just a humble servant. I serve not out of duty, but out of love. I am free to leave at any time, but I choose to remain because I am treated with respect and kindness. Other households have asked me to serve them, but I have refused on each occasion because their intent and interest was for me to serve their ego needs, that is, for them to be seen in the city as worthy of a servant such as me.

"The role of the servant is a powerful one and not understood by many other servants, as well as masters. A servant provides services to a master and determines how he will be served. He can withhold or share as he sees fit. He can serve with love or serve with resentment. He can serve unconditionally or with strings. The servant who serves without strings attached will find peace and harmony. The servant who serves out of duty only will find anger, resentment, blame, and an empty heart.

"Permit me to give you an example of that which I speak.

"Many years ago when I was a child, my father was a servant to a cruel and selfish master. At our mealtimes, my father would often speak of the injustices, but always in a kind and loving manner. I often asked him why he continued to serve in this household. His answer was always the same.

" My son, I have chosen the role of servant. I am here in this place at this time for a reason. To learn, to grow in wisdom and understanding, and to find inner peace and balance regardless of what my outer circumstances may appear to be. This is not always an easy task, however, I have learned that while I am the servant I am also the master."

"What do you mean father?"

"My son, you are young and may not understand my reasons, but I will share them with you so you might ponder them as you grow in maturity, self control, and years. A servant determines what and how his master will be served. He is in control of the amount of, and quality of service that he provides. This is truly a position of power. The master, on the other hand, when he asks me for his meal or his saddle or whatever his request, must wait for me to respond. Is that not a position of weakness? Is not my position one of power? Does that not make me the master and him the servant?"

"Father, I do not understand your reasoning. You are still the servant, and must respond to the demands or requests of your master."

"Yes, my son, but I can do them with love, or I can just do them. Does that not also give me the power?"

"I still do not see your point father."

"There is more to giving service than the service itself. The most important condition of providing service is in the attitude of the server. I lose power to my master when I permit him to influence my attitude about myself, and my role as his servant. I keep my power when I serve with love, no matter what his expectations, methods, and attitudes. We all serve some master, my son. Some serve in the city, and some on the caravans, some in the temples, and others on the seas, other still serve the merchants. Your mother serves you, and I serve your mother. Am I her servant? Is she yours? I think not. But we do serve.

'There is service to, and a servant of. I am a servant of, but choose to see myself as offering a service to.'

"Many years later my father's master passed away, and when his final words were written it was discovered that he left all of his property and wealth to my father. When my father passed on several years ago he left all of his wealth to me."

It was Ahmed who spoke. "What is your name?"

The servant answered, "Lasib."

"Lasib, if you have such wealth, why are you a servant, and why do you not live in your own home with servants of your own?"

"Sir, you have missed the meaning of this important Scroll. Why don't you share with your friends your interpretation of its meaning."

As the servant left, Joseph had a smile on his face as he winked at the departing Lasib.

"Ahmed, we are waiting."

"And wait you shall. I do not agree with the message in this Scroll."

"And what is it you do not agree with?" Asked Haroun.

"First of all, I must tell you I am not pleased with the impertinence of this servant. I know I am a guest in your chamber, but I have traveled over the mountains and through the cities and have never had a servant take that tone with me."

"Are you objecting to his tone or manner because of his role as a servant or because of his role as a fellow traveler through life?"

"What do you mean?"

"You too, Ahmed, are a servant. do you agree?"

"Yes, but......"

"Please let me continue. You will have your chance to respond. I think it is time for a break, my friends. Let us take a walk through the city and have our noon meal at one of the cafes. There is something I would like all of you to see."

Chapter Eleven

We started to leave, and as we walked through the high arch that served as the entry-way, to the inn, Haroun turned and asked Lasib to join us. He agreed and our small party began the short walk toward the town square where the merchants were selling their wares. We entered a small but comfortable café, and the owner gave us a large smile and greeted us warmly.

"Welcome, ladies and gentleman, to my humble cafe. Please make yourselves comfortable."

"We ordered a beverage and had spent several minutes in idle conversation when the owner appeared to take our order.

When we all had ordered our lunch, Joseph picked up the conversation where we had left it.

"Ahmed, do you not see yourself as a servant?"

We all half-listened as Ahmed explained his position and views on the servant/master roles. When he was finished, our food arrived and we all ate. During lunch, the cafe owner told us there was a visitor inquiring earlier about our group, and that he wanted to know if the owner knew the purpose of the gathering and whereabouts of the meeting. The café owner said that he expected us for the noon meal, and if the visitor wanted to meet our group to return later in the day.

The café owner continued, "He is here now, sitting over in the corner observing and listening."

None of us had noticed the man, but now that we were aware of his presence, we all noted that there was something familiar about him. It was Haroun who left the table and approached the man. We could not hear the conversation, but the stranger looked visibly angry and unsettled. Haroun then sat next to the man as they continued their conversation. He was gone for several minutes before he returned to our table to share their conversation with us.

Haroun began. "The stranger is from the west many days ride. He is one of the teachers of the first twelve Scrolls. He has recently heard of the newly discovered twelve Scrolls, and has many misgivings about their authenticity, purpose, and value. He says that selling in the caravans and in the cities has never changed, and that we are wasting our time discussing the new Ancient scrolls. He says he has read the second set of Scrolls, but will not tell me where or when. he apparently knows them because he shared the thirteenth and fourteenth Scroll with me.

"Why do you suppose he has traveled far? not just to tell us of his disagreement with these new Scrolls? And how does he know of them?"

"No, I believe it is his intent to destroy them. The Scrolls Thirteen through Twenty-Four that are in my possession are the originals, and there was apparently one copy, which he says he has read and destroyed. This is what he has told me."

Just at that moment we all looked over at where the stranger was seated and noticed he was gone, as if he had vanished into thin air.

Haroun said. "Do not fear I have locked the Scrolls in my secret vault, and if he chooses to steal and destroy them he will have a difficult time about it. Please continue enjoying your lunch. I have a short errand to attend to. I will return shortly."

After we had finished our lunch, Haroun returned and said, "there is something I want all of you to see. Please follow me."

We left the cafe and began to walk toward the desert away from the city. We approached the remains of what appeared to be an old castle in the middle of the desert. As we neared what was once the main entrance, we heard an explosion that came from the direction of the inn. Everyone in our group seemed concerned except Haroun.

"Do not worry, my friends, the explosion you have heard is of no consequence. We have much more important things to focus on. Please let us continue. there is a tomb, recently unearthed, that you must see before we continue our discussion of this Scroll."

We began our return trip to the city in silence. No one could speak after witnessing what we had seen in the tomb.

Each of us had seen many miracles and mysterious events during our lives, but the experience we witnessed at the tomb was beyond our wildest imagination.

As I went over the sequence of events again and again in my mind, I still was unable to comprehend its magnitude. My life would never be the same again.

Many of the details were now buried in my consciousness, but one overriding fact stood out. We had crossed over to the other side of some barrier, and entered an entirely new reality. I am not certain whether the barrier was a physical one or only psychological. It no longer mattered. What we saw would challenge our view of the present, and the future for the rest of our days.

Once on the other side, our bodies lost their physical form. we were both the whole as well as a separate part of the whole at the same time. Our thoughts, as well as the thoughts of every living soul past, present, and future, became instantly known to each of us. There was a tremendous feeling of love, peace, and unity there. The sounds and sights were familiar as well as unknown at the same time. None of us spoke. We were all astounded by what we saw. It was a scary yet comforting feeling. It is hard to explain. None of us had ever experienced anything like it or ever read anything in the ancient writings of such a phenomenon. What was the purpose of this place or time or whatever it was. And why did Haroun want us to see it now? I was confident that we would soon have an answer to that question.

Chapter Twelve

When we reached the edge of the city, we could see a large crowd of people who were passing water buckets from person to person. The line ended at the Inn where Haroun was staying and the Scrolls were hidden. We all gasped - as the Inn was in flames and appeared to be a total loss.

Joseph spoke hurriedly, "The Inn, that must have been the explosion we heard."

Haroun, in a rushed voice said, "let us see how we can help."

We all pitched to help extinguish the flames and tend to the injured. Fortunately, the Inn was almost completely empty of its guests when the explosion occurred, so very few people were hurt. No one was killed, but there were several badly burned peasants who were passing by at the time.

"The Scrolls," screamed Aziza, "the Scrolls are destroyed! What will we do......"

Haroun interrupted, "do not worry. while you were finishing your lunch, I quickly returned to the Inn and removed the Scrolls and placed them in my vault in my caravan leader's tent. They are safe. I recognized that man instantly in the café. He has a reputation throughout the land as a charlatan and trouble-maker. He disguises himself as a teacher, one interested in Truth; but in fact, he is a fake. By his presence here, I anticipated some evil deed; however, I didn't believe he would go this far to destroy the Scrolls. It is a safe assumption that he is well on his way beyond the city and that any chance of apprehending him would be slight. We must do what we can to help the injured and then return to our discussion. It is evident that there are those who would destroy what the Ancient twelve Scrolls represent. We must hurry and complete our discussion and understanding of the Scrolls so we can each be on our way."

Joseph said, "we can conclude our discussions in my home. Let's meet there in one hour and conclude our discovery of the final five Scrolls."

Haroun answered with, "I will pick up the Scrolls on my way."

Our group, which had grown to nine with the addition of Lasib, settled in at Joseph's home.

Haroun took charge of the discussion, "let's continue where we left off. We were concluding our thoughts on the nineteenth Scroll - Service.

"Haroun, what was the purpose of showing us the ancient tomb after lunch?"

"Thank you for bringing that up, Mahmoud. I believe we can conclude our discussion of this Scroll with an explanation by me of why I wanted you to be a first-hand witness to the experience each of you had at the tomb. Then we can move on to the final Scrolls."

"Please begin. we are all anxious to hear your explanation," offered Aziza.

Haroun began slowly, "I first discovered the tomb several years ago while returning from visiting a very ill friend. He had only a few days left in this world, and asked me if he could share a secret with me. I said yes. He began, 'Haroun, there is a legend about an ancient tomb that was the burial site of one of the original Seers. It has been passed down through the ages that this Seer came from another world. He knew things about the future that no one, in their wildest mind, could ever imagine.

'I went to the tomb late one evening and saw a beam of light coming right through a solid stone wall that housed the tomb. When I approached the light, I saw that there was an opening, like a small crack in the wall that, was permitting the light through. Suddenly the stream of light stopped, and I was bathed in darkness. I became very afraid, but stayed to observe what might happen next.

'The legend has also claimed, that on the eve of the 7th full moon of the new year, one person from this side is permitted the opportunity to visit and observe what is on the other side. Now, Haroun, all this talk of the other side was quite strange to me and I never paid it much heed, however, my curiosity had finally given me the courage to see for myself.

'My visit took place on the Eve of the seventh full moon almost fifty years ago. I have told no one of my discovery since that time. I was afraid I would be called a lunatic, and locked away for all my remaining days.

'Anyway, let me continue my story. I peered into the crack and saw what appeared to be miniature planets and moons swirling rapidly around in a circle. The next thing I knew I was on the other side witnessing an entire new dimension of reality. I couldn't believe what was happening.

'I saw things, Haroun, scary things in the future that to this day I have been unable to understand. I have searched all the writings from the past, and have found no evidence of such a reality anywhere

'I saw things, Haroun, scary things in the future that to this day I have been unable to understand. I have searched all the writings from the past, and have found no evidence of such a reality anywhere. I want you to further investigate my discovery before it is too late. There must be at least one other reliable witness to validate my finding so that I can share my experience with the world before I pass on. Will you do that for an old friend, Haroun?"

"Of course."

"Well my friends, I did visit the tomb last year on the eve of the seventh full moon and had exactly the same experience that each of you had today. Let me do my best to try and explain what I believe we all saw.

"There seem to be parallel realities, or dimensions that exist simultaneously. We are currently in one of many of these realities. Now there seems to be no time, as we know it, in many of these other dimensions. So it is possible that in one such reality, The inhabitants could be living in our future 5000 years from now: or in another, living in our past, several thousand years ago. Now when I say our past or future, I do not mean to imply that we are seeing our futures or our past.

"What we are seeing are entire other worlds made up of inhabitants from another time and place. These worlds could represent our future and/ or our past, and there is no way of knowing, with our limited view of our lives. The ancient writings are not complete in many ways. And the Seers view of the future, as far as we know, is limited in many ways.

"Let me conclude. What I believe each of you saw was a peek into our own future, and the role that each of us will play in the destiny of mankind. I further believe that. when we complete our discussions of the Scrolls, we will each in our own way, be shown what our destiny is, and how we are to fulfill it.

"I believe this because each of us was given access to the other side. Not just one of us as the legend describes. We are all supposed to be a witness to this unusual phenomenon for a reason. I believe it must have something to do with the scrolls."

Chapter Thirteen

"Let us move quickly to the Scroll marked number Twenty. Safia, will you read this Scroll for us?"

"It is my pleasure, Haroun."

She began, *"The Scroll marked number Twenty is about Integrity. It says that integrity is one of the highest forms of service you can offer your fellow man. It is living your life from the highest perspective possible. It is sharing Truth with others at all times regardless of the difficulty or pain it might cause you or the others you share it with.*

"It goes on to explain that this pain is far easier and better in the long run than the pain of deceit and dishonesty. Dishonesty is only a result of a lack of Integrity. Integrity is not an action to take or a belief that is held. It is a way of life. It is the standard by which you measure all of your words, actions, commitments, and behavior. It is not something you have when it is convenient or easy.

"A person with integrity says what he or she feels or believes And behaves consistently with his or her words. Since everyone's truth is a perceived truth, it is often difficult to know whether a person is close to the Truth. The one way to determine this is to test it against the one true measuring device - does it do harm to any person, in any way, at any time? Now again, harm is a perceived interpretation, so we must have a common understanding of the concept of harm. Does it in any way inflict damage to another person or group - emotional damage, physical damage, or psychological damage? Granted, each of us has unique feelings and attitudes about everything. But a person with integrity integrates this understanding and awareness into each transaction and action.

"Integrity is one of the soul's main desires. The soul strives to help us live with integrity by sending us signals when we are acting in a way that is out of harmony with everyone's highest interest. These signals may be physical signs from one's own body, or signals from the universe that can take many forms. But rest assured when you act without

integrity, there will be signs, and there will be consequences if you ignore the signs. That is all there is about integrity."

"Thank you, Safia. who will begin our discussion on integrity?"

"I will Haroun," replied Mahmoud. "I believe integrity is showing your true colors even when you are confident that no one will ever know or discover that you took an action that seemed to lack integrity. I can think of one example that comes to mind from an experience King Harold had several years ago.

"When he was interested in having some work done on several of the rooms in his new castle, he contacted a merchant who specialized in castle decorating. The merchant made recommendations that he thought would be acceptable to Harold. Harold is not big on show, so he trusted this merchant to give him the best advice on how to achieve the look he wanted without appearing overly extravagant or outrageous.

"The merchant told Harold what he thought he wanted to hear even though he knew at the time that what Harold was trying to accomplish was impossible. Harold purchased his services. The work was complete, and when Harold inspected the result he was disappointed in the workmanship and feel of the rooms that were done. When he contacted the merchant and asked for an explanation, this is what the merchant said," King Harold, I knew that what you were trying to accomplish was impossible, but I thought you would be happy with the results.

"It is not possible to achieve the look you want with the materials that are available today. We had to make substitutions, and these substitutions changed the feel of the rooms."

"How did the King respond, Mahmoud?"

"He asked the merchant to redo the rooms at his own expense. And when he was finished, he told him that he was considering redecorating 50 additional rooms in the castle, but he would not give this business to him. He would locate another merchant with more integrity, Even if he had to transport a merchant from far beyond the horizon, and give room and board to him and his family, and workers for the entire time they were working on the castle. He also told him not to use him as a reference, as he would tell the merchant's prospective customers of his experience. Furthermore, he would never give the merchant any referrals, so he need not ask."

"That merchant lost enough business to last him the rest of his career because of his lack of integrity."

"Does anyone else have a story to tell, or further interpretation of the message in this Scroll?"

"Yes, Haroun. I have just a simple example but one that has far reaching consequences."

"Let us hear it, Joseph."

"I have a policy in my business that I want my customer to be 100 percent satisfied with whatever merchandise he or she buys from me. This policy is well known throughout the city and beyond. For years I never had anyone ask for a refund.

Then one day a stranger approached my stall in the market, and asked to return a vase he had purchased from me a year before while he was visiting the city. I did not recognize the man or the vase. It is also not typical of the type of merchandise I sell. I asked him why he wanted to return it, and he told me he purchased it with the understanding that it was an original from the castle of the retired King Asib.

"He told me it was a fake, and that King Asib never owned such a piece. He could not produce evidence that he purchased from me. Now what do I do? Do I trust him? Do I challenge his presumptions? Do I deny that I ever sold him this piece? Do I give him a credit towards another piece of merchandise? I must admit my first reaction was to tell him I was sorry that I could not take the merchandise back."

"What did you do Joseph?"

"Well Ahmed, I told the man I would be happy to give him a full refund, and that he could pick out something else from my inventory for no charge in exchange for his trouble."

"What did he say?" asked Ahmed.

"He said that would not be necessary. he did not want to gain at my expense. And then he purchased half of the items I had in stock. He gave me several hundred gold coins for the merchandise, and asked if I could arrange to have it delivered to his castle. I said that I would be happy to. That was the biggest sale I have made to date since I began my business several years ago. I later discovered that he was King Asib himself."

"And he didn't tell you that in the beginning?"

"No, he acted like a common peasant. It appears that he might have been testing my reputation of integrity. I suppose I will never know."

"That is an excellent story for our other merchant friends to hear. It re-affirms the importance of maintaining integrity at all costs and the potential of good for all involved.

"Let us move on, if we may, to the next Scroll, number Twenty-One. Who would like to read this one? Kahlil, what about you? you have been quieter than I have ever known you to be."

"I will be happy to read the next Scroll, Haroun."

Haroun handed Kahlil the Scroll marked Number Twenty-One.

Kahlil began, "This Scroll is about Trust, it reads as follows: *Trust is one of the vital issues in all successful relationships. Without trust, relationships are doomed to fail. Trust is built slowly over time, and can be destroyed in an instant. Trust is the result of acceptance, integrity, forgiveness, truth, honesty, openness, and a set of standards that are agreed upon by all parties in the relationship. When any of these standards are violated, trust breaks down, and the relationship will begin to erode. This erosion may take months, or even years, but in reality the day the erosion begins is the day the relationship ends.*

It is possible to begin to rebuild trust in a damaged relationship caused by this issue, but both parties will always retain the memory of this broken trust. This does not mean that the relationship cannot ever get beyond this issue, only that it will take time and healing. Most people are unwilling to give this rebuilding process the time it takes, or have the patience to work on the issues that caused the relationship to break down in the first place. It concludes by saying, that trust is a factor of many other issues, and is not a stand-alone issue."

"Does anyone know why this Scroll comes so late in the Scrolls since it seems to be related to many of the other ones?"

"I believe," began Lasib, "that a merchant must be willing to comprehend and master the other eight Scrolls in this second set, and that if he can, trust is a by-product of this understanding and mastery."

"What do you think, Ahmed?"

"Haroun, I have always believed that trust is an important ingredient in any relationship, but I am not sure why it is covered so late."

"Any thoughts, Lasib?"

"There are many kinds of trust. There is the trust you have of your wife or husband to be faithful. There is the trust you have of your employees to be honest. There is the trust you have of the process of your life as it unfolds, that you are where you are supposed to be, and doing what you are supposed to be doing at the time. That there are no accidents in the universe, and that the divine plan of God works its good for all even though we cannot either understand or see the future outcomes of our present actions and decisions.

"There is the trust you have of yourself that you will do and say the right things at the right time, so you can grow and contribute to the growth of another. There is the trust we have in God that our life is perfect in every way. There is the trust we have in each other to share that which will help us become more aware and learn. So as you can see, there are many things, people and events to trust. I have only mentioned a few as time is growing short."

Chapter Fourteen

"Does anyone have anything to add to this discussion of trust?"

Aziza began, "Yes, Haroun, I would like to tell you all of an experience I had several months ago while visiting a nearby city. It began very early in the morning. My husband had just left on a caravan to pick up a load of merchandise and supplies for his business. It was going to be a very long trip. I would not see him for several months.

"I hated these long trips of his. We were new residents in this city, and I did not know many people. I felt alone and often afraid. As you know, it can take weeks to receive a letter from many of the other cities. Often I would not hear from my husband at all while he was away. Well, let me get to the heart of my story.

"After watching his caravan leave, I stood for several minutes as I watched them disappear into the glaring sun. It was then that it happened. I had this premonition that I would never see my husband alive again. I was frightened, and did not know what to do.

"A voice from somewhere in my head spoke, 'do not be afraid Aziza. Your life is your own to do with what you choose. Although you are married to your husband, you have an independent life of your own. You share a bed, meals, dreams, fears, and plans with him, but you also must have your own dreams and plans. You and he are connected in many ways, but you are also separate. You must learn to trust that all that happens in your life happens for the best, if not now - then later. eventually, everything works in conjunction with divine guidance. You must learn to trust this unfolding. do not judge by appearances, rumors, or the messages that are often sent to you by your ego. Trust yourself. Trust, Aziza, and you will live a long and happy life."

"My husband never returned. I learned from a passing traveler that his caravan was attacked by bandits, and all were killed. I learned shortly thereafter that I was with child. I did not know how I would ever be able to support my child with no skills, no family, and no friends in the city, but I believed in the voice, wherever it came from, that all would be well. There is more to this story, but I will save that for later if we have time."

"There are many travelers through life that have similar fears, Aziza. These fears can take many forms. The fear that they will not do well in a new career, business or relationship because of past mistakes. There is a wise old saying that says, - *Forget your mistakes but remember their lessons* - This saying continues – *Your past does not have to become your future unless you let it.* I believe this is sound advice for many weary travelers through life who are in need of encouragement, support, and confidence. Let us move to Scroll Number Twenty-Two. Khatib, would you please do the honors?'

Khatib began, "*Scroll Twenty-Two deals with wisdom. It begins, Wisdom and knowledge are two different things. Knowledge is awareness of, where wisdom is the use of what you know. There are many things you know that you are not aware you know. There are also many things you don't know that you are not aware you don't know. Although this might seem confusing to some people, we will simplify it. Knowledge is not power, the use of knowledge is power.*

"*The ultimate goal of gaining wisdom must come first through your search for knowledge, whether from inside your consciousness or the world but regard-less of its source, knowledge is the door to wisdom. On the other side of this door is the ability to know what to use, and when to use that which you know.*

"Many people have knowledge but lack wisdom. Wisdom softens the soul while knowledge alone can attempt to harden it. The soul seeks only for the conscious awareness of the wisdom it knows you already have. The true goal of wisdom is awareness. The soul knows. Wisdom Is. Knowledge is potential wisdom, and only matures through experience, or the use of, the knowledge gained.

"Your purpose for gaining knowledge is to un-learn that which life has taught you that is not in line with the soul's wisdom. This may sound unusual, this unlearning, but rest assured, your soul knows what you need to know to be happy, productive, and joyous. It concludes by saying, seek not only knowledge, but the understanding of that knowledge, so you can apply it to the circumstances and conditions of your life."

"Very well done, Khatib. Let us begin our discussion. Who would like to begin?"

No one spoke for several minutes. It was evident in the silence that none of us were quite sure as to the true meaning of this Scroll. We had all learned that knowledge was supreme. Now we were discovering that knowledge, in and of itself, has no value. This idea was in contradiction to the teachings of all the prevailing scholars of history.

Haroun asked again, "will someone respond to this Scroll?"

"Haroun, I will try," offered Mahmoud. "For centuries, many merchants had awareness of the first Twelve Scrolls, but did not practice their teachings, and suffered as a result. The elder who had access to them for many years and never even read them died a broken lonely man with a crumbling church that no one ever visited.

"He had the opportunity to put the teachings of these Scrolls to use, but he believed that only merchants in the marketplace sell, that elders do not sell. It is obvious that he did not understand the true meaning of the words, *to sell*, and that is - to influence and persuade. If he had read the Scrolls and put their lessons into practice he could have helped so many weary travelers on the highway of life."

"That is a good analogy, Mahmoud. Would anyone else like to offer an idea?"

It was joseph, who had been quiet for a long time who now spoke, "I have learned that even little children have this ability to influence and persuade. They may have never seen the First Twelve Scrolls, but nonetheless, they are effective at persuading. They get what they want, one way or another.

"Now, I am not suggesting that merchants use some of the techniques used by children, but there is a lesson here. They have wisdom without knowledge. That explains some of the wisdom in this Scroll."

"An Excellent analogy Joseph. is there anyone else who would like to comment?"

"I have a question, Haroun. I still do not understand the difference between knowledge and wisdom."

"Let me see if I can clarify this for you, Safia. Knowledge is the accumulation of information. Wisdom is the ability to know what information you need to acquire, and, once acquired, when, and how to use it."

"Very good, Ahmed. Is everyone clear on the meaning of this Scroll? Can we move to the second to the last Scroll now - Number twenty-three?"

"Can we take a short break first, Haroun? I need to stretch and get some fresh air."

"Let's resume the discussion of the last two Scrolls after a short break. Is that acceptable to you all?'

We all nodded in agreement. As we left Joseph's house, one of his children approached and asked Lasib, "Lasib, I though you were a servant. why are you here meeting with my father? Is he going to hire you?"

"No my son, I am here at the invitation of life."

"What do you mean the invitation of life?"

"Let me see if I can explain. Life comes to each of us one moment at a time, day-in and day-out, until our final day on this Earth. Each of us is presented each moment with decisions, options, or choices as to what we will do with what life puts in our path. Some of these choices and the decisions or actions we take will have life-long impact on us, while others are just the trivia of the moment.

"When life gives us an invitation to participate - whether in a sport, activity, discussion, relationship, business or any of the thousands of opportunities we have - each moon cycle, we can choose to get involved, or we can turn our back. We can participate, or we can ignore the invitation. Each of us, even you son, are given opportunities or invitations from life each day. What have you done with yours today?"

"Well Lasib, I was given the opportunity to ask you why you are here, and I chose to take life up on the invitation and ask you. I could have ignored this opportunity and let it pass."

"Very good. I believe you know now what an invitation to life is. I am here because life invited me, and I chose to participate."

With that, Lasib walked out into the sun and joined a few of us who were enjoying the many gifts of life.

"What a beautiful day," Khatib said. "It is days like this I am glad to be alive."

A discussion followed with Khatib and Mahmoud.

"Are you saying, Khatib, that on less beautiful days you are not glad to be alive?"

"No, but I can see the reason for your question. I love every day. it is just when everything seems so right, it is good to be alive."

"Do not be lulled, my friend, into the thinking that life is only good when things are right. There is much to learn and gain from life - when, to use the opposite of your phrase - when things are not right."

"The universe does not know right and wrong, good or bad, better or worse, happy or sad. The universe and everything in it just is. No judgments, no expectations, no hurry, no mistakes, and no sadness or happiness. Over the long term The universe is not swayed by our human attitudes, feelings, concerns, or fears. On the short term, each of us brings into our life that which is consistent with our thinking over time.

"This consciousness is part of the divine universal consciousness. Let me give you an example. Place a drop of colored dye into the ocean, and it disappears into the wholeness of the ocean. It is still there, but you cannot see it. With time if everyone every day for generations put colored dye into the ocean, eventually the ocean would become the color of the dye, but it would take thousands of years. This is what is called reaching critical mass or a concept that was revealed many years ago by a famous seer, called, the hundredth monkey theory."

"What is the hundredth monkey theory?"

"It would take too much time to explain it now. Let us save that for another time, my friend."

The rest of our group joined us and Haroun said, "Let us return to our final discussion, my friends."

We all took our places around the trunk for the last time. I was sorry to see our discussions coming to an end; yet I was anxious to return to Harold to tell him of my journey. I did not achieve what he sent me after, but I believed my mission was successful.

Haroun said, "I will read the second to the last Scroll." He unrolled the Scroll and Read slowly, *"The Twenty-Third Scroll is about Belief. There is a new world coming. Not only in the physical sense, but in the spiritual sense as well. The old rules of human interaction will no longer apply to relationships, transactions, business or career success, or any other area of life. It is essential that anyone wishing to master the wisdom found in these final Twelve Scrolls, must totally understand, accept, and apply the message in this Scroll every day of his or her life.*

He continued, *"Belief is the foundation for all success, whether in the real or metaphysical world. Belief is the starting point of all that follows, whether for good or for evil, for the benefit of man or the destruction of him. Those that believe strongly can work miracles. Those who have weak beliefs seldom achieve success and those that completely lack belief inherit the results of that state of mind, nothing worthwhile. These people contribute very little if anything to the positive destiny of man. Hear us messengers, You must instill a strong sense of belief in those whom you teach. You must convince them that a strongly held belief, put into practice through decisions and action can stand against any obstacle, any fear, and any failure or disappointment."* He concluded, *"Belief is the foundation of all that has been, is, and will be.*

What did the scroll mean, Hear us, messengers?

Chapter Fifteen

Haroun said, "I will begin this discussion. Many merchants have lived and operated under the old cliché that has been passed down through the years, 'Fake it until you make it.' It is unfortunate that these merchants never stopped to challenge the wisdom of this saying. they took it for what it was worth without question. As a result, many merchants failed, because this became a way of life. They lived with this attitude for so long that they came to believe that their act was really who they were.

"What they failed to understand was that their customers, family, friends, and associates saw through this act. Some merchants, however, never believed this old saying and developed authenticity. They were real. You knew who they were. They did not build walls around themselves. They let people know them, their fears, frustrations, hopes, and dreams. As a result, these merchants had satisfying relationships with their customers, family, and friends and anyone who crossed their path. They learned that self-disclosure builds bridges in relationships and a lack of it creates barriers.

"There is only one true path to freedom, and that is through humility. 'The humble will inherit the Kingdom' was penned by an old priest many years ago. This does not mean to imply that humility is a sign of weakness. Quite the contrary. it takes a very big person to have the courage to be humble.

"There is another way to look at the ideas in this Scroll. Belief is a habit of action. You get what you believe in sooner or later. Sew incorrect beliefs, and you will gain incorrect results. Sew correct beliefs, and you will benefit from positive outcomes. I want to ask you to consider another way of looking at this. Suppose you believed you were going to fail. Now failure is not a negative thing. It can be another opportunity to learn. 'You must fail often to succeed sooner', a wise teacher once said.

"But, let us for a moment see this failure as negative. A merchant who believed every day when he went to his stall that this was going to be another bad day on the way to his ultimate failure, would attract the events, circumstances, and results that this thinking encouraged. Think of the mind as a magnet. As we move through life we attract those people, circumstances, and events that are consistent with the dominant thoughts we hold in our minds.

"This does not mean that to be a successful merchant only requires you to sit in your stall thinking positive thoughts. One of the old Seers years ago said, 'pray but move your feet as well,' if you hope to succeed.

"The real question here, my friends, is: what if all of this metaphysical, spiritual, and emotional stuff has no basis in truth, and, in fact it doesn't matter how you think? That you in no way influence the quality of your future by how you think, what you believe or how you feel? Why bother developing a strong belief system? just continue faking it.

"Why even fake it if this faking has no bearing on the quality of your life?

"This is precisely the point. If it doesn't matter, you have nothing to lose by controlling your thoughts. The question is: do you enjoy your present moments - and these are the only ones you have - more because of this type of positive thinking? Having said all of this, I would like to conclude that I have seen enough evidence in my life that right thinking does matter. people who are happy, productive, and feel a sense of joy and gratitude do more, have more, contribute more, learn more, use more of what they have, and pass from this world content that their life had meaning. And what more can we ask?"

"Haroun, I believe you have very eloquently summed up the wisdom in this Scroll, but I would like to add one thing."

"What is that Mahmoud?"

"Harold sent me on a mission several moons ago without instructions, guidance, or a plan. He only told me what outcome he wanted. I wasted a great deal of time before I realized that I did not understand my lack of success. I lacked belief in my mission, myself, and my ability to fulfill it. I wandered for weeks from city to city and caravan to caravan. each day ended in despair and frustration. I now see that I needed to experience those emotions in order To gain the understanding that I have in our discussions. When I return to Harold, I will not have fulfilled his mission: however, I will return with even better news. I have gained new wisdom from the second set of Ancient Scrolls."

"Would anyone else like to comment on the meaning of this Scroll?"

"I believe we are all in agreement with you, Haroun. We see the wisdom in belief, the purpose of controlling thoughts, and their contribution to our lives."

"Thank you Safia, then let us proceed with the last Scroll, Number Twenty-Four."

Haroun carefully removed the ribbon from the Scroll and slowly unrolled it. He sat there for several moments staring at the Scroll with a shocked look on his face.

"What is it?" asked Mahmoud.

Haroun did not respond, but rolled up the Scroll and passed it to his right to Lasib. Lasib unrolled the Scroll, Appeared to read it, paused and rolled it up, and handed it to Ahmed. This process continued until it reached me, sitting on Haroun's immediate left. I unrolled the Scroll, read and I was stunned. I rolled up the Scroll, placed the ribbon around it, and handed it back to Haroun.

After several minutes Haroun finally spoke, " what do you all think?"

Epilogue

No one spoke for several minutes.

"Please." Haroun asked, "what do you all think?"

We were all stunned at what we read.

"Very well," Haroun responded, "I will read this Scroll."

"It Says,

Faith is all you need.

Haroun, Lasib, Ahmed, Safia, Aziza, Khatib, Joseph, Kahlil, and Mahmoud...

...End your discussions now, go in peace, and share the message and meaning of the Ancient scrolls with mankind."

The order our names were written on the scroll was the same order we were seated in the circle around the trunk!

And there was also something else very curious. Scrolls thirteen through twenty-three were all written in blue ink, meaning that someone had previously read these scrolls. But the last one, number twenty-four, was in red ink. If the legend was true, all of the scrolls had been read but the last one. We were the first ones to see this message!

No one spoke. Haroun replaced the Scroll in the trunk, locked it, and stood. "My friends, thank you for your time, insight, sharing, and love. We will now go in peace, and change the world.

"Good bye, my friends, until, and if, we meet again in this life. Enjoy Peace, love, and safe travels.

"Share your message with passion and commitment; Knowing that your mission is blessed by God."

We all embraced, and slowly left Joseph's home one by one.

None of us ever saw each other again, but word spread rapidly from sea to sea of our success at sharing the wisdom of the Second set of Ancient Scrolls with travelers everywhere.

However, our work had only really just begun.....